D1134994

"I found myself chuckling and groaning in equal measure at Caitlin's misadventures. Brimming with playful language and guided by a strong, distinctive voice, *Boat Girl* is a buoyant read that's sure to find a berth in readers' hearts." —**BRUCE HALE, AUTHOR OF *SWITCHED* AND THE *CHET GECKO MYSTERIES***

"Elizabeth Foscue's *Boat Girl* glows with all the glories and the hilarious pitfalls of teen life in a contemporary Caribbean paradise. Transplanted unwillingly from Annapolis to the British Virgin Islands, Caitlin Davies navigates it all with only her brilliant, naïve, wisecracking, pop-culture-savvy mind on board to guide her through first love, shrimp bites, and scruffy villains. A great summer read no matter what time of year you pick it up." —**D.J. PALLADINO, AUTHOR OF *WEREWOLF, TEXAS* AND *NOTHING THAT IS OURS***

BOAT GIRL

ALSO BY ELIZABETH FOSCUE

PEST

BOAT GIRL

A Misadventure

ELIZABETH FOSCUE

⁺ KEYLIGHT
B O O K S
AN IMPRINT
OF TURNER
PUBLISHING

KEYLIGHT BOOKS
AN IMPRINT OF TURNER PUBLISHING COMPANY
Nashville, Tennessee
www.turnerpublishing.com

Boat Girl: A Misadventure

Cover design by Faceout Studio
Book design by William Ruoto

Library of Congress Cataloging-in-Publication Data

Names: Foscue, Elizabeth, author.
Title: Boat girl : a novel / Elizabeth Foscue.
Description: First edition. | Nashville : Keylight Books, an imprint of
  Turner Publishing Company, [2023] | Audience: Ages 12-16. | Audience:
  Grades 7-9.
Identifiers: LCCN 2022048672 (print) | LCCN 2022048673 (ebook) | ISBN
  9781684429448 (paperback) | ISBN 9781684429455 (hardcover) | ISBN
  9781684429462 (epub)
Subjects: CYAC: Moving, Household—Fiction. | Popularity—Fiction. |
  British Virgin Islands—Fiction. | LCGFT: Novels.
Classification: LCC PZ7.1.F6715 Bo 2023 (print) | LCC PZ7.1.F6715 (ebook)
  | DDC 813/.6—dc23/eng/20221219
LC record available at https://lccn.loc.gov/2022048672
LC ebook record available at https://lccn.loc.gov/2022048673

Printed in the United States of America

For Mary, Hank, and Chris Foscue.
And for *Whither Bound*, long may she float.

BOAT GIRL

CHAPTER 1

On the plane
11:14 a.m., August 10

[Note: This all began in May, so I'll have to start there. This wouldn't make any sense otherwise. Not that I plan to let anyone read this—ever—but if the tabloid parade of former Disney stars has taught us anything, it's that stuff we mean to keep private can be our express ticket to internet infamy. And I can't afford Miley's PR team.]

B ut aren't there pirates in the Caribbean?" Shelby asked.

Shelby has been my best friend since fourth grade, but she's not too concerned with the issues of our day. Which is not to say she's dumb—this girl can balance chemical equations in her head faster than Mr. Murphy can write them out on the Smart Board—but current events aren't her thing. She won't even watch *The Daily Show* with me anymore because she could never tell when Trevor Noah was kidding. She would raise her hand in Civics and be all, "Well I happen to know that Mitch McConnell drinks puppy blood," and then Sister Ann would give her detention. (I don't know whose idea it was to let a nun teach Civics. As a rule, nuns aren't much for free and open debate.)

Anyway, the closest thing to news Shelby watches now is *Daily Pop* on E!, so I wasn't surprised by her question.

"There are no pirates," I answered.

Shelby wasn't convinced. "I know I just saw something about pirates on TV."

"That was *Pirates of the Caribbean.*" We'd watched the movie at Shelby's house because, thanks to my parents, we remain the only family on the planet without Disney+. Shelby's parents are actually present, so they don't have to ban perfectly unobjectionable media platforms to feel like they're doing a good job. Although her mom can be a little weird about refined sugar.

"Oh, ri-ight," she breathed, "with Orlando." Her eyes glazed over and she was gone, off to Shelbyland, where circa 2003 Orlando Bloom was urging her to lay all her love on him on a Mediterranean beach. This *Mamma Mia* sequence is Shelby's favorite fantasy, and other than the frequent recasting of the Dominic Cooper part, it hasn't changed since she first adopted it in seventh grade. She's been humming the song nonstop for, like, *four years.*

In this case, though, I thought Shelby might have miscast Orlando. He seems too dignified for that big, flipper-clad musical dance number.

I guess Shelby had that problem, too, because Orlando barely had time to belt out the first verse before she blinked and asked, "And you're sure no pirates? Because that would be awesome."

"Pretty sure," I said. Although, she was right; that would be awesome.

Not *real* pirates, obviously, because real pirates were terrifically bad people. But Shelby and I binged *Once Upon a Time* last summer and, you know, I could really get behind a swashbuckling Killian Jones or two. Oh, and maybe an Errol Flynn. I watched an Errol Flynn movie with my grandma once and was much impressed. Errol swashbuckled at least as well as Hook and didn't blame all his problems on a disembodied hand.

"Well, even without the pirates," Shelby said, "I still don't get why you're so upset about this. I think moving to the British Virgin Islands for a year sounds cool."

I stared. "How can you say that?"

She rolled her eyes. "Stop being so fear-of-changey for a second and think about it. It's the Caribbean. Clear, blue water. Warm weather *year-round*. Palm trees. Frosty drinks. Not to mention the hot island boys."

I snorted. "Great, then I'll have Annapolis boys *and* island boys ignoring me."

"Not true." Shelby wagged her finger. "You get to start fresh with the island boys. They haven't known you since forever. You'll be new and exciting. I mean, who knows what you could do without all this baggage."

"Hey," I said, stung, "I've done plenty."

Pfft. *Baggage.* I've been working since the first day of ninth grade to scrabble out a niche for us at school, and it hasn't been easy. The rigidness of the social hierarchy at Our Lady of Perpetual Sorrows rivals that of the Catholic Church—and those crusties have been working on *their* flowchart for over two thousand years. You might, in fact, call OLPS "cliquish." And there is nothing—nothing!—more fraught in such an environment than an extracliqueular existence.

Sure, Shelby and I have each other, but two measly people cannot populate a lunch table. So the successful completion of my sophomore year at Our Lady of Perpetual Sorrows—and by "successful" I mean "didn't have to embrace social reject status and join Music Ministry"—had only been accomplished through painstaking strategy on my part. And I do mean painstaking. The odds had not been in my favor.

First of all, I am almost two years younger than everyone else in my grade. (Early August birthday + addiction to educational apps = permanent alienation from peers.) After Sister Brigid, the principal of the Lower School, made me skip third grade, I finally learned to lay off the ABCya! But the fact remains, I will be a fifteen-year-old junior for the entirety of the upcoming school year. And I'm not the kind of fifteen-year-old who can pass for sixteen, either. Seriously, I'm lucky to pass for twelve. I'm five-foot-one, skinny, and my hair is the same strawberry blonde it's always been, which is a nice color for a five-year-old, but ten years later? I look like an overgrown American Girl doll. Plus, unlike most girls my age, I have not shared in the benefits of the whole hormones-in-the-chicken phenomenon, because my mom will only buy organic.

Another obstacle to my assimilation has been the very thing I admire most about Our Lady of Perpetual Sorrows, namely its high level of organization. Students are always accounted for, lunch breaks are staggered, hallways are monitored—it's the Swiss watch of schools. But all this structure effectively rules out the time-honored method for avoiding social scrutiny: hiding out in the library. And if you can't hide and you can't fit in, it's only a matter of time before you find yourself playing keyboard accompaniment to "Our God Is an Awesome God" during Friday mass.

After much deliberation, Shelby and I had come up with a new approach. No existing clique would have us (okay, they would have welcomed Shelby with open claws, but she says she's not a joiner) and we were categorically unwilling to cry defeat. (Unwilling *and* unable. Apart from the fact neither of us plays an instrument, Shelby doesn't even eat the cracker.) So we'd created an entirely new class of student: we are The Fixers.

All that stuff student council is supposed to do but doesn't? That's what we do. *We* got lunch catered by Moe's. *We* carved funding for the drama club out of the engorged lacrosse team budget. *We* got an extra two minutes between classes added to the schedule (so that now it's theoretically possible to stop for a pee without being marked tardy).

Some question our methods, but we are not the talking heads who read morning prayer over the PA and lift up glitter glue as their false idol. We are the behind-the-scenes masterminds who bring about real change. We are a necessary evil; popular nowhere, tolerated everywhere.

"I didn't mean it that way," Shelby said. "I like what we've got going, too. But . . . umm . . ." She picked at her thumbnail, which she only does when she's thinking something she doesn't want to say.

"What?"

She hesitated, then looked up at the ceiling. "The thing is, I remember what it's like to be, you know, one of the in-crowd. I like how we are now *better*, but at least I got to make an informed choice. You never got to try out . . ." she shrugged apologetically but said it anyway, "normal."

Her eyes dropped back to my face, gauging my reaction.

I gave her a reassuring smile. I mean, really, it isn't news to me that I'm a total freak. But I did have to correct her on one point.

"Shelby. Come on. There is no way in this universe I could pass for a normal eleventh-grader. Anywhere."

She pursed her lips. "You could if you wanted to."

"No. Really. I couldn't."

Truly, I am the worst teenager ever. It's like everything I do is too young or too old. I don't listen to the right music, or watch the right shows, or laugh at the right jokes. Rule-breaking makes me nervous, learning makes me happy, and the *endless* gossip makes me want to impale myself on a tetherball pole. (I mean, really, why am I supposed to care about whatever nugget of hate speech Nicky Boucher dropped on her cross-country teammates *this* week? If they had any sense, they'd all just stay away from her like I do.)

"Well," Shelby said, "I think you could at least fake it. With a little effort, you could probably convince them that you're normal"—she waved her hand with a flourish—"*for an American.*"

Well with that kind of encouragement, how could I fail?

"Just don't tell them how old you are," she added.

"Uh-huh," I said. "Well, how about we focus on this stuff first and maybe save ourselves the effort of planning Operation: Not a Freak?"

"Oh." She blinked. "Sure. What are we looking for, again?"

A reasonable question. The Maryland Law Library is not one of our usual haunts, even though it's only a short bike ride from my house. But I had a plan.

"We're trying to find out if I can sue for change of legal guardianship." I flipped through the index of the *Maryland State Code, Annotated*, searching for the words "minor" and "custody."

"You mean, get some guardians other than your parents?"

"Exactly. If you can believe it, it's perfectly legal for parents to *force* their children to leave the country of their birth. And I don't have time to lobby our congressman or whatever. So I'm just going to replace my parents," I explained.

Something I'd always secretly wanted to do. On a trial basis, of course. Just to see.

"Oh," she said. Then, "Hmm." She picked at her nail again.

"What?" I asked.

"Nothing."

"No, really. What?"

"Well," the Machu Peach-U nail polish she'd applied that morning in Religion was peeling under her prolonged assault, "if your parents aren't your guardians anymore, someone else'll have to be, right?"

"Yeah . . ."

"Well, I was just wondering . . ."

"What? Just tell me!"

She gave a little huff. "Okay, well, how are you going to get someone to be a guardian to *you*?"

"Oh." A point I hadn't considered. I thought about it for a minute. "Maybe your parents?" I suggested.

Shelby gave me a pitying look and shook her head. "Not after the thing with our attic."

"Your room feels much more spacious with the vaulted ceiling."

"And our Wi-Fi mesh."

"Hmm . . ."

"*And* the thing with the Historical Socie—"

"Alright! Fine," I snapped.

Shelby's parents aren't the most organized people on the planet. I, on the other hand, have a certain talent for order and optimization. Unfortunately, Mr. and Mrs. Willett have never really appreciated my efforts on their behalf. And it's totally not my fault that they bought a house without getting the ceiling joists inspected, but whatever. Moving on.

"If they didn't have to assume legal responsibility for me, do you think your parents would let me stay with you for the year?"

"Oh." Shelby looked away. "Umm. Mayyyybe."

Good enough.

If I couldn't get the state to intercede on my behalf, I would have to turn to a higher power. Luckily, Sister Philomena was in her office.

"Oh, Caitlin Davies. I thought I might see you today. Come right in."

Her words were polite and welcoming, but I wasn't fooled. Sister P is a lot like a polar bear, and not just because of the snowy white

habits all the nuns in her Order wear. You know going into any encounter with Sister P that she's dangerous, but you get so distracted
by her serene face and competent manner that you don't even realize
she's snuck around behind you. Then, before you know it, she's rolled
a boulder onto your head and squashed you flat, like an unwary seal.

Scary stuff.

I actually have a lot of respect for Sister Philomena. Upper School
at OLPS starts in seventh grade, so I've had four years to observe her
methods, and she's impressed me. She runs a tight ship. She doesn't
take it very well when other people try to improve on her systems,
though. She's kind of a control freak that way.

It was that inner control freak that I was counting on today.

Sister P's office is pretty small—it might actually have been a
closet or something at one point, though it does have a window—so
I more or less slid into her visitor's chair from the doorway.

She barely glanced up from the task before her, which involved
a red felt-tipped pen and a press-ready draft of the Upper School
newspaper.

"What can I do for you?" she asked, marking a big red X through
an article titled "Gym Students Protest Violation of Locker Privacy."

Like I said before, free and open debate is not really a core tenet
of Catholic schools.

I took a deep breath and, not bothering to hide my urgency,
asked, "Sister, have you heard?"

"About your family moving to the British Virgin Islands for a
year? Yes. Your parents came in to see me yesterday. I hear you'll be
living on a sailboat." The red pen struck again. "How exciting."

"Huh." Not the response I'd been hoping for. I had imagined
that, once Sister heard I was going to go slack around in the Caribbean for a year, she would rise up in holy fury and forbid my parents
to remove me from school.

Okay, she probably can't forbid them to take me, but she could at least threaten to not readmit me for senior year. My mom wouldn't care, but my grandparents would.

If my mom had gotten her way, I'd have gone to public school, where you have to carry a clear plastic backpack so security can see if you're carrying hookah pipes or nunchucks or anything. My grandparents pretty much had a cow when they heard about this, though, and insisted on bankrolling Our Lady of Perpetual Sorrows so my mom couldn't turn me into an atheist.

My dad was raised Catholic and he says it didn't leave much of an impression but, in the end, my grandparents convinced him. He talked my mom around by pointing out that if I went to Our Lady of Perpetual Sorrows, I could walk to school, which would teach me self-sufficiency and environmental awareness, and (I suspect this was the clincher) they wouldn't have to worry about pick-ups and drop-offs.

Of course, since fourth grade, I've only walked as far as the end of my street, where I've hitched a ride with Shelby and her dad in their Volvo SUV. But my mom doesn't know that.

Catholic school can be awful, especially when they make us get confirmed or attend school baseball games, but the public schools in movies look insufficiently organized for my taste, and anyway, where do you hide tampons in a clear plastic backpack?

"Sister, you're not really going to let them take me, are you?"

"Why, Caitlin, I think it will be a wonderful experience. It will look excellent on your college applications. And I'm sure I'll find *some* way to hold things together in your absence."

Apparently, sarcasm is not considered a sin. I wracked my brain for another angle.

"But, Sister, you've only got two more years to mold me into a proper Christian soldier. I have to build up enough moral fortitude to last me at least through college. If you let them take me to live among the Godless heathens now, my soul could be lost forever."

Sister P rolled her eyes. Yes, nuns do that, too.

"I hardly think the people of the British Virgin Islands qualify as Godless heathens, Caitlin. In fact, your parents described it as a very Christian, family-oriented country."

I swear, my parents will do anything to get their way, even manipulate a nun. It's shameful. I bet they don't even know—and certainly don't care—anything about the religious habits of British Virgin Islanders.

I shook my head slowly. "Sister, I'm afraid it won't be enough. There will be *nude beaches*." Those were all my grandad could talk about after he and my grandma took that cruise to St. Maarten. "And, umm, carnivals that don't stop. And you know my parents don't go to mass. I think I'd better stay here, don't you?"

"Hmm." I could tell Sister was much struck by the reminder that my parents are the biggest Godless heathens of all. "You may have a point."

Yesss. Victory! With effort, I kept a concerned look pinned to my face.

"Well." With the red pen, she made a note on her desk calendar. "I'll just have to call your parents in for another chat."

I was ready to dance around my chair, until she continued, "They're planning to send you to the local high school on Tortola. But after this conversation, I think the private school they mentioned would be a better option. St. Hilda's, I believe it's called. It's Church of England, I'm afraid, but in this case, I think we'll just have to take what we can get.

"Besides"—she shot me a smile I knew well—"I think your soul will be safe enough there." I shivered as the shadow of a boulder fell across me. "St. Hilda's is girls-only."

Squish.

CHAPTER 2

Still on the plane
12:26 p.m., August 10

Oh *come* on. They call this a tapas box? It's stale pita chips and some gelatinous sludge labeled "Asiago Spread" in a fancy takeout container. Hey, United Airlines: Cheez Whiz by any other name is still Cheez Whiz. Yech. There are no depths to which airlines won't sink.

Anyway, back to my story.

At this point, some girls might have given in gracefully. You know, before they made things worse. Not me, though; I'd worked entirely too hard securing my place in this God-blessed heaven hole to lose it now. I know it might sound like my life in Annapolis isn't all that great, but it could be much, much worse.

I could be like Karlee Catton, who Nicky Boucher and Bea Bustamonte tormented every day *for a year* in Economics—just because she refused to do their Mock Stock project for them. Karlee transferred to Annapolis Christian Academy and had to quit sailing, because ACA doesn't allow students to play sports on Sundays. No one's seen her since. Or I could be like Griffin Kant, whose unfortunate last name led to a nickname so awful that I can't even *write* it, because what if my grandma or someone got ahold of this journal? (See former Disney stars.) Poor Griffin even got kicked out of Music Ministry, which is supposed to be the last stop, accepting of all comers. (Except I can totally see why they had to let him go. The senior boys pretended to be huge fans and chanted his name every time he took the stage—hardly the sort of thing you want happening during school mass. God won't stand for that kind of nastiness.)

High school is the event horizon of humanity, and I know better than anyone that Karlee's and Griffin's fates could easily have been mine. And they still might be. I have no idea what social disasters await me at St. Hilda's.

It was all so dire. I'd just gotten my life sorted, and my parents were blithely ruining everything. Their callous disregard for my well-being was truly appalling. Over the next month, I tried repeatedly to speak truth to power, but to no avail. It was clear they'd been plotting in secret for some time. I mean, I seriously doubted my dad's sabbatical from Johns Hopkins was approved overnight. He even had a contract for his book proposal.

And, as for my mom, she wasn't just taking a year off, she was *retiring*. From a job with a federal pension! So, okay, I got that her job as an emergency department doctor was stressful, but she hadn't even *tried* normal coping strategies, like adult coloring books or wine. Abandoning her career and forcing the whole family to adopt a nomadic existence in a foreign country struck me as a gross overreaction.

Since he tends to be the reasonable one, I cornered my dad alone in a last-ditch effort to save us all.

"Look, Caitlin, she can't keep doing this. She's been on call every other night for the past month."

I mean, yes, that's awful. But . . . "That's kind of the nature of the job, though, right?"

"Well, no, that's the thing." He scrubbed a hand over his jaw. "They're not hiring enough providers. She's burned out. She needs a change."

She only missed my entire childhood for this job, but okay. I moved on.

I had low expectations for any attempt to reason with my mom and I was right. She insisted this would be "a priceless opportunity for us to experience the world and *really connect* as a family."

No, I promise, she actually said that.

I'm already sufficiently connected, thank you very much, although there is no denying that my little brother, Finn, could use some attention. He was suspended twice last year. From preschool. *Montessori* preschool. At the rate he's going, he'll be wearing his First Communion suit to his first sentencing hearing. Still, it is painfully obvious that the child doesn't need this kind of upheaval in his troubled young life.

And I have to wonder if my mom is truly prepared for all that the full-time parenting of Finn will entail. The adoring little cherub she encounters on the rare evenings and weekends that she isn't on call bears little resemblance to the vindictive hell spawn the rest of us endure. (Just ask those poor Montessori teachers.)

Anyway. Despite my parents' obstinance, I stuck to the plan and soldiered on. Unfortunately, my presentation, "Skin Cancer Incidence in Pale Families Who Foolishly Dwell in Equatorial Climates," only earned me a wardrobe of Coolibar sun-protective clothing. Pretty cool—if you're a Jawa. And when I discovered that reef fishes in the Virgin Islands often carry ciguatera, a build-up of neurotoxins that they can transfer when eaten by humans, causing serious neurological issues, my mom grounded me from using JSTOR. She said it was making me paranoid.

I needed a new plan.

~~~~~~~~~~~~~~~

O ne day in late June, as my August departure date grew inexorably closer, Shelby and I sat in front of Storm Bros. while I buried my sorrows in a waffle cone of German chocolate cake. It was my third cone of the day, but I'd found that the freezy goodness somewhat soothed my broken spirit.

"You need to look at this as an opportunity," Shelby announced, licking delicately at her cone of caramel truffle.

"Oh god," I groaned. "Please don't start again."

A duck wandered over and fixed its beady eyes on my waffle cone. Shelby shook her paper napkin at it, and it waddled backward a few paces. "Look, don't you ever want more out of life? More than negotiating with nuns for out-of-uniform days?"

She said that like it was an easy task but, believe me, it's not. Nuns have answered a calling that requires them to wear uniforms *every day for the rest of their lives.* They aren't particularly sympathetic to teenagers' desire to wear jammies to school in honor of Homecoming Week.

Shelby snapped her fingers in front of my face. "Focus. Isn't there anything you dream of doing?"

I glared. "Yes! Winning the—"

"*Other* than winning the Microsoft Excel Olympics."

"It's the Financial Modeling World Cup," I muttered.

"Seriously, Caitlin, this is your chance to shake things up. Have some fun."

"We have fun." The duck inched forward again, and I eyed it warily.

"Don't be disingenuous."

Shelby had used the word "disingenuous" three times in the last hour. Her boyfriend, Carson the Tech Crew Boy, had gifted her a

Word of the Day calendar to celebrate their three-week anniversary. For Shelby, three weeks is an impressive milestone; she goes through a lot of boyfriends. Not because she's clingy or attracted to jerks or anything. All of her boyfriends are very nice. That's kind of the problem.

Shelby just wants a nice boy to go to the movies with her and maybe show off for her on his skateboard when she's bored, but the guys she dates usually end up declaring their love for her in the first week or so. Then she has to dump them because she's just not looking for a serious relationship at this juncture.

But Carson the Tech Crew Boy was breaking all the records. Oh, he was in love with her, all right—boys who aren't in love don't celebrate three-week anniversaries—but so far, he had managed to contain his rapture. Carson was playing it cool.

Every time I start to feel bummed that guys never ask me out, I comfort myself with the knowledge that at least I don't have to pretend to be excited about stuff like Word of the Day calendars.

"What I mean," Shelby continued, "is this is your chance to experience your teenage years as they are meant to be experienced."

Oh, who am I kidding? I would love the heck out of a Word of the Day calendar.

"And how would either of us know how our teenage years are meant to be experienced?" I asked.

"I've seen all the movies," she said, which was not an exaggeration. Shelby soothes her sugar-deprived soul with screen time. "Think *To All the Boys I've Loved Before*," she instructed knowledgeably. "Think *Clueless*. Think *Mean Girls*."

"You want me to push someone in front of a bus?"

"Shut up. You know what I'm talking about."

"Not really, but—Get out of here!"

"Huh?" She shot me a startled look.

"Sorry, I was talking to the duck." Who, in an alarming shift of interest, was now eyeing my flip-flop-clad toes.

"Forget the duck," Shelby complained, her toes safely ensconced in a pair of neon green Vans. "What you need is to be the star of your own movie. And not a movie about waging a political battle or organizing the leftovers in the fridge, either. You need to be the star of a *good* movie."

I broke a slab off the side of my waffle cone, held it high for the duck to see, and tossed it as far as I could. It landed at the paws of a leashed black Lab, who chomped it down instantly. The duck and the dog's owner both glared at me.

"Shel," I said, "I am not the kind of girl who stars in good movies. Or any movies."

"Why not?" she demanded.

"I'm weird."

"It's all about presentation. From now on, you're 'quirky.'"

"I'm fourteen."

"No one has to know that."

"I'm short."

"So what? Guys don't care. That just makes it easier for them to look down your shirt."

I snorted. "Like they'd bother." I have nothing of interest in that region. To such an extreme that, as Wyatt Guffy is fond of telling me, the wall is jealous.

She glanced at my chest for a long moment. "Like I said, it's all about presentation. We just need to do a little shopping."

"I'm scrawny."

I've always been scrawny, but the scrawniness hadn't become a remarkable feature until the other girls in my grade—Shelby included—all filled out in interesting ways. And if you think uniforms can level *that* playing field, you've obviously never worn one.

Nothing looks worse sticking out of a plaid kilt than a pair of pale chicken legs.

Shelby patted my knee. "Have another ice cream."

~~~~~~~~~~~~

W e spent the next month preparing for Operation: Not a Freak. Shelby took me shopping twice: once to find a bra that "makes the most of what we're working with" and again, just a few weeks later, for pretty much a whole new wardrobe. Because, as it turns out, she was right about the ice cream. I ate so much that I finally kicked the kids' department and graduated to an adult size 0. My mom had to let me buy all new stuff, and Shelby appointed herself my stylist.

Shelby says there is a crucial difference between the Catholic schoolgirl look and the Christian schoolgirl look and that, until I grasp the difference, I am forbidden to pick out any of my own clothes.

Like I'm really going to sneak off on my own to raid Brandy Melville, but whatever.

We also watched a lot of old TV shows starring girls as shiny as Shelby and guys who were even bigger clown trucks than the boys we have at Our Lady of Perpetual Sorrows. Those shows kind of freaked me out, truth be told. It had never occurred to me that there might be schools even more ruthless than OLPS.

"*No place* is more ruthless than OLPS," Shelby assured me half-way through *Pretty Little Liars: Original Sin*.

"Someone on this show got murdered."

"Yeah, well, I've Heard Some Things about the senior retreat," she said.

Neither of us really knew what my life would be like in the BVI—the Wikipedia page didn't have much to say about youth culture—but Shelby explained everything I was learning was broadly applicable, suited to most teen environments.

"Beyond that, we'll just have to tackle situations as they arise," she said. "Don't forget to keep your phone with you." As much as my parents embraced the "Wait Until 8th" propaganda, they'd been forced to buy me a cell when I was ten because they kept forgetting to pick me up from sailing practice and I'd needed a way to order Ubers. Other than arranging rides, I didn't use the phone much because the only person I talked to was Shelby and we were always together. That would have to change. Remote Shelby was better than no Shelby.

We'd also gotten permission for Shelby to visit me over Christmas break so she could evaluate my progress and help me with any necessary damage control.

It wasn't a great plan, but it was the best we could do.

~~~~~~~~~

Yesterday, my last precious day on native soil, I stopped by Our Lady of Perpetual Sorrows to collect my transcript from the main office. I guess Miss Patty, the receptionist, gets summers off, too, because Sister Philomena herself emerged from her closet and found the folder for me.

I was pretty chilly to her because, hey, she left me hanging when I needed her, then got me sent to an *all-girls* school. Sister P didn't seem to notice, though—or if she did, she didn't let it bother her.

She handed me a little package wrapped in sparkly tissue paper. "I got you something for your adventure, Caitlin."

I felt the shape of a book through the wrapping. It wasn't thick enough to be a Bible, so I guessed it was something like *Prayers for the Catholic Traveler* or *The Grisly Death of St. Agnes, Patron Saint of Young Girls*.

"Oh. Wow."

"Make sure to take it with you and use it every day. I can't tell you how much I regret not having one when I visited Rome a few years ago."

Definitely the traveler's prayers, then. Yay.

"I will, Sister. Thanks for the present."

Then I went home and wrote her a nice thank-you note because, I mean, so what if it's lame? A gift is a gift and manners are manners. And it's not like nuns are exactly rolling in dough.

Then I forgot all about that tissue paper package until oh-dark-thirty this morning, as we headed off to the airport. I was busy sorting through the travel documents, making doubly sure everyone had their passports, with photocopies packed separately (as recommended by the US Department of State) and prescriptions to go with all the medications.

"What's this?" my mom asked.

"It's a present Sister P gave me for the trip."

"Oh! Well, why haven't you opened it?" Nothing, I repeat, nothing, excites my mom like a wrapped present.

She didn't deserve a treat, but I needed to check all the luggage tags, so I said, "You can open it."

Doctors, even retired ones, open presents with surgical precision. She had the tissue undone in seconds.

"Oh, how thoughtful."

I shifted Finn, who had fallen asleep on top of a large Rubbermaid bin, and taped a second address label to the lid, just in case.

"Matt," I asked my dad, "is the back door locked?"

"Hmm. I'll check." He ambled off toward the back of the house.

"Caitlin! This is so sweet. I don't know why *I* didn't think of getting you one," my mom gushed.

"What? Why would you buy me a prayer book?" I asked. She was working hard to de-stress, but she hadn't let Jesus take the wheel or anything. In fact, she seemed to have gone the other direction entirely. She'd bought Birkenstocks and an essential oil diffuser, and I'd seen her reading something called *The Path of Druidry: Walking the Ancient Green Way* on her iPad.

But when I turned, I saw it wasn't a prayer book at all. It *was* a book, but instead of saints or glowing doves on the cover it was decorated with a world map, and engraved on the cardboard spine were the words "Travel Journal."

I shrugged. "Stick it in my backpack," I said.

And I'm so glad I did. Journaling will be great practice for writing my memoirs one day (after finishing my appointment as secretary of state.) And writing in this allows me to ignore my dad, who pulled out cards and a cribbage board as soon as we reached cruising altitude. Why can't he just drink rum like all the other adults on this plane?

Oh, wow, there are islands out the window!

CHAPTER 3

The Pickled Pirate Hotel & Pub
9:10 p.m., August 10

U p to this point, I haven't been very excited about the whole "living in the Caribbean" aspect of this fiasco. I mean, I've seen four seasons of *Survivor* and, frankly, the tropics never looked that enticing.

But landing in St. Thomas was pretty cool. Even from the plane I could see palm trees and green mountains and shining blue water. Seriously, the water here has me gobsmacked. Annapolis is a big sailing town, so I've pretty much grown up on the Chesapeake Bay, but the Chesapeake is *nothing* like the Caribbean. The instant I stepped off the plane, a wash of hot breeze whipped my hair out of my scrunchie and filled my lungs with damp, salty air.

Salt-scented breezes never blow through the streets of Annapolis. Probably because if the Chesapeake had a signature fragrance, it would be Washed Up Crab Trap. I've been told that the reason the Chesapeake is so murky is because it has a "live bottom." I'm not entirely sure what that is, but the only life I've noticed are the fat ducks that swim around the harbor eating discarded ice cream cones and the occasional horseshoe crab. And I think horseshoe crabs can survive in nuclear wastewater. Probably the ducks can, too.

Since St. Thomas is one of the United States Virgin Islands, we didn't have to go through immigration when we got off the plane; we would do that in Tortola. Instead, all deplaning passengers filed past the Welcome Cart, which looked like those fancy wooden trailers at the Maryland Renaissance Festival, except it was painted with a cheery island mural instead of "$5 Madame Misty sees your past, present, and future $5."

A pretty Black lady with a tray of little paper cups stood by the Welcome Cart handing out fruit punch. She gave me a cup as I walked past, then gave my parents some punch off a different tray, which seemed to make them very happy.

We proceeded to the baggage claim, where we found the carousel still and empty, so I pulled out the luggage manifest I'd printed out the night before and a pen, and stood at ready.

Ten minutes passed.

My dad, who was already starting to sweat on account of the baggage claim area not being air-conditioned, went off to buy a bottle of water.

After another ten minutes, I was sweating, too—so much so that my jeans stuck to my butt and thighs. This was a serious development. Prolonged wearing of wet jeans can cause a very unpleasant condition, known to seasoned junior sailors as "Alligator Ass." Shelby got a bad case of this in fifth grade after sailing the Oxford Regatta in a pair of jean shorts, and it took two weeks and a tube of prescription steroid ointment before she could wear a bathing suit in public again.

With doctors for parents, I have easy access to prescription steroid ointments, but still . . .

"What's the holdup?" I asked my mom, who seemed perfectly cool in one of her new gauzy mystic-tree-hugger ensembles.

"What, the luggage?" she asked absently. "I wouldn't worry about it. It'll come sooner or later."

I eyed her askance. If you asked me, she was going way overboard with this whole lifestyle makeover. And "sooner or later" wasn't going to cut it. We had a ferry to catch. "But it's been half an hour since we got off the plane."

"Caitlin, things down here happen on Island Time."

Oh. Well, someone should have told me. That actually made sense, when I thought about it. We'd been on that plane for hours, long enough to pass through three or four time zones, at least.

I took off my watch. "How do I adjust for Island Time?"

She shook her head. "It's not a time zone. It's . . . well . . . it's an abstract concept that describes a more relaxed lifestyle."

Uh-huh. "And what, exactly, does that *mean*?"

She gave me an exasperated look. "It means sooner or later. Here"—she shoved a box of crayons at me—"why don't you help your brother color?"

"Erica, I have to go potty," Finn informed my mom.

Shelby thinks it's weird that Finn and I call our parents by their first names, but they never bothered to refer to each other as "mommy" and "daddy" so we never learned to, and after all, those *are* their names.

"Sure, baby," my mom said. "Caitlin, have you got this under control?"

By "this," I guess she meant our fourteen separate articles of checked luggage. The lady at the United Airlines desk had made my dad fork over a doozy of an extra luggage charge.

"Sure."

When Finn and my mom returned, there was still no sign of our luggage or my dad. I made a big show of checking my watch.

"Hmm." My mom glanced serenely at the inactive carousel. "It's bound to come soon. I'll just go find Matt." She wandered off, Finn in tow, leaving me alone with the potential luggage again.

Of course, as soon as she left, things happened all at once. A buzzer sounded, the carousel lurched into motion, bags began shooting out from behind the rubber flaps, and suddenly I couldn't pull our stuff off the belt fast enough. My parents came running over, and between the three of us, we managed to collect everything on my manifest. While they stacked bags and bins on the luggage cart, I trotted over to the woman with the clipboard who runs the taxi stand and told her we needed to go to the ferry dock in Charlotte Amalie. Her eyes glittered when she heard how much luggage we had.

"It's three dollars for every bag," she said.

"That's fine," I assured her. My parents could afford it, and besides, they're the ones who let Finn pack his entire Paw Patrol collection.

It occurred to me that I hadn't seen Finn for several minutes.

"Erica," I called to my mom, "where's Finn?"

"What do you mean, where's Finn? I left him with you!"

"No, he went with you to find Matt. He was right behind you!"

We left my dad to haul the luggage out to our designated taxi and went hunting for Finn. I wasn't all that worried. Experience has taught me that Finn is pretty easy to find. I'm not sure if it's the bright red hair, or the arresting air of malevolence, but no one ever forgets seeing Finn.

And because of the whole biting thing (cause of preschool suspension #1), he's an unlikely candidate for kidnapping. His little teeth are wicked sharp and he knows how to use them.

About five minutes later, I spotted Erica walking over to the taxi with Finn cradled in her arms like a limp baby.

"Is he okay?" my dad asked, alarmed. "Where was he?"

My mom looked grim. "You know the Welcome Cart, where we got punch when we got off the plane?"

"Yeah."

"Finn was behind the stand drinking his way through an extra tray of rum punch."

We all stared down at Finn, who cracked one eye and gave us a lazy smile.

"Bad Finn," I said.

"He's not going to be sick now?" the taxi driver asked in alarm. "This truck is brand new!" He was a heavyset Black man wearing a shirt with a tropical sunset print. His nameplate introduced him as Forbearance, and his van was indeed very nice.

"Nah," my dad said. "Don't worry, I'm a doctor."

The airport taxi stand was a marvel of efficiency. I was truly impressed. The woman with the clipboard jotted down where everyone needed to go, then put groups of people headed in similar directions in the same taxi.

This caused some grumbling among the other passengers, especially those who were riding in taxis so crowded that their luggage had to be tied to the top of the vans, but it was effective organization at its finest. I took notes.

Because we had so much luggage—more than they could tie on the roof, even—we got our own taxi. This cost a lot more but turned out to be a good thing because we had to stop a couple of times for Finn to throw up.

Despite the frequent stops, we got to the ferry dock in Charlotte Amalie with time to spare. Forbearance made up time for all the barf-stops by ignoring red lights.

While we waited for the ferry, I stood at the edge of the dock and stared out over the harbor, marveling at the activity. Sailboats, yachts, ferries, and what appeared to be a floating restaurant all maneuvered around each other in an orderly fashion. At one point, a floatplane landed in the middle of it all (without crashing or squashing anything, much to Finn's disappointment) and taxied over to a building beside the ferry dock. At the far end of the harbor, three cruise ships, shaped like shoe boxes and sized like small planets, formed a neat line along a concrete quay. And the water . . . it was just incredible, the exact aqua of Aquafresh toothpaste. It was all I could do not to jump right in.

I mentioned this to my dad, who laughed. "This is just a dirty harbor," he said. "Wait until you see the clean stuff."

Our ferry, a big metal boat called the *Bomba Charger*, ran non-stop to West End, Tortola—our final destination. The ferry had two levels: a downstairs, which was enclosed and air conditioned, and an upstairs, which offered metal benches fitted to the roof of the first level, with a railing around the edge to keep people from falling overboard. My dad looked like he might have enjoyed some time in the a/c, but Finn was still looking a little green, so we climbed the steps to the top level.

Finn lay with his head in my mom's lap as the ferry roared out of St. Thomas Harbor. My dad helped my mom scrub at a Finn-barf stain on her tunic with a baby wipe. I started to offer them my stain pen, but then I looked up and forgot everything.

My dad was right about the water. As soon as we cleared the harbor, cloudy aqua gave way to crystal-clear turquoise, bleeding to pure blue where it deepened or amber gold where it broke gently over rocks and coral reefs. As we picked up speed, a cool breeze ruined the ponytail I'd just finished redoing, and a slender gray bird, which my dad called a frigate bird, appeared by the side of the boat. I watched it carefully in case it decided to fly over the ferry and poop on us, but it seemed happy just to glide along as we followed the rocky coastline.

My guidebook had names for the individual islands we passed—St. John, Buck Island, Goat Island—but the mountains, sun-drenched green and shadowed purple, seemed to belong to one long, curvy landmass.

I read my dad a page of the book that claimed when Columbus "discovered" the Virgin Islands back in 1493, he thought they looked like a bunch of virgins, hence the name. I've been surrounded by statues of virgins since kindergarten and I couldn't see it, but my dad said it was because Columbus had been at sea too long. Even for an undersexed Catholic dude—and I know because I go to a school full of them—that seems pretty pervy.

There were roads and fields carved into some of the mountains, and houses perched on some of the hills, but mostly the mountainsides were wild and green, the coastlines dotted with big, gray boulders.

We passed sailboats and motorboats and, on one memorable occasion, another ferry whose wake caused ours to roll alarmingly to one side. I grabbed the rail, but Finn didn't even twitch. Finally, we rounded a rocky point and pulled into the most gorgeous little harbor I've ever seen.

The water in this cove is much bluer and clearer than the water in Charlotte Amalie, and there are no cruise ships at all, just lots of sailboats. One side of the harbor is called Frenchman's Cay. It has a small marina and a row of little buildings painted bright, happy colors with metal roofs and gingerbread trim. There's even a clock tower. It's like something out of a picture book.

In contrast, the other side of the harbor has a squat, two-story cement building painted an ugly maroon color. Completely charmless. Naturally, that's where the *Bomba Charger* docked.

"Here, you carry Finn," my mom instructed, plopping my brother in my dad's arms. We joined all the other passengers swarming off the boat and entered the squat building, which turned out to be Customs and Immigration.

The customs official eyed our mountain of luggage with suspicion.

"This all belong to you?" he asked my dad.

"Yes, indeedy," my dad answered, handing over our customs form.

The customs man glanced down at the form. "You are vacationing here? All of these things will leave with you at the end of your stay?"

"Yep," my dad confirmed inaccurately.

I knew immediately what had happened. We are not, of course, here on vacation, and most of our luggage is stuff for the sailboat we'll be living on. We plan to sell it along with the boat at the end of our year here.

But my dad, you see, had not understood the question. He grew up in Tennessee and, as a result, can't understand anyone who isn't from the Deep South or reporting news on NPR. We can't even send him to Baltimore County without an interpreter, and he's lived in Maryland for twenty years. I don't know how he functions when he's teaching. I guess he doesn't take many questions. Anyway, Virgin Islanders have a *completely* different accent than we do, which, to my dad, is completely indecipherable.

I didn't want the customs man to think we were lying to him. He couldn't possibly have believed my dad; normal tourist families do not travel with mountains of luggage.

Nor do they pack in large plastic boxes. At that very moment, the man was resting his hand on a Rubbermaid bin that—I discreetly consulted my manifest—contained four new pillows and a fire extinguisher.

I couldn't exactly stand there and let my dad go to jail for smuggling.

I turned to the customs man and said, "Sorry, sir, he has trouble with . . . uh . . . English. Most of this is stuff for the boat we're going to live on."

"Oh?" He turned to my dad with an unfriendly look. "If you are importing these things into the BVI, you must pay duty on them," he said. "Open all these boxes, please."

Oops.

After we'd repacked the boxes and paid the customs man a lot of money, we lugged our stuff out to another taxi, which drove us maybe an eighth of a mile down the road to a place called The Pickled Pirate. Our hotel for the night.

The rooms at The Pickled Pirate aren't anything fancy, but they fly a Jolly Roger out front and have a restaurant that makes exceptional nachos. I will survive. We'll only be here a couple of days, after all.

My dad was already sitting at a table with a plate of nachos in front of him when I finished showering and wandered out. My mom, who'd been putting Finn to bed, trailed behind me, baby monitor in hand. "Well, he's asleep," she sighed, checking the screen as she settled into a chair.

"You mean passed out?" I asked, nabbing a chip.

"Quiet, you," my dad said. "And put down that nacho. After what you just cost me in import duties, we can't afford to feed you for the next two weeks."

Jeez.

I took myself over to the bar, where I ordered my own nachos and spent the rest of the evening writing in this journal and watching ESPN on the bar TV.

I hate sports.

CHAPTER 4

The Pickled Pirate
2:54 p.m., August 11

This morning, my mom took me to visit St. Hilda's, my new school. I won't say I was *excited* about previewing the site of my upcoming estrogen-drenched downfall . . . but I was a little curious. I mean, I've been at OLPS since kindergarten. That's eleven years in the same school, with the same people. I like predictability more than just about anybody, but that's a lot of sameness.

And, okay, we had an orientation when we moved from the Lower School to the Upper School, but that was mostly to acquaint us with the expanded version of the Student Handbook. (Rules in the Lower School are classroom-specific and follow a general "naughtiness makes Jesus cry" philosophy, whereas the Upper School administration has codified misbehavior in exhaustive detail.) We traded our jumpers and Peter Pan collars for kilts and regular oxford shirts. We traded cubbies for three-hundred-pound backpacks. The nuns got a little more arbitrary. Other than that, not much changed.

But I could tell, even before I got out of the taxi, that St. Hilda's was going to be a change and a half. For starters, the campus is waterfront. A waterfront school! I mean, there's no lounge chairs or cabana boys—I guess that would be kind of distracting—but it's *right on* the ocean. The school buildings sit just in front of a wide AstroTurf athletic field, and beyond that—*bam!*—panoramic views of the Sir Francis Drake Channel.

Back in Annapolis, there would be trillion-dollar condos and a Marriott on this kind of land.

A robust-looking white lady named Ms. Gibson met us out front and introduced herself with an English accent as the "headmistress," which made me kind of nervous. I've never seen that word used anywhere but Roald Dahl books and, just to be clear, if this turns into a *Matilda* experience, I'll *swim* home to Annapolis.

I probably won't need to, though. Ms. Gibson seems super nice. Her accent had me expecting Lady Mary to join us for tea at any moment, but she was casually dressed in khaki cargo shorts and an athletic tank. She wore her hair long—almost to her butt—in a style Shelby would call "Earth Mother Chic." I caught my mom eying Ms. Gibson's graying tresses as she ran a quick hand through her own cropped, I'm-a-doctor-with-two-kids-and-no-time haircut.

Well, she certainly has time now.

Ms. Gibson led us through the main entrance and into a spacious, sunny office. Instead of the conventional desk and spartan visitors' chairs, Ms. Gibson's office had a wide couch and a couple of papasan chairs. The walls were covered with abstract paintings, framed photos of girls' sports teams, and Caribbean Pride posters. Knickknacks with a student-made look about them adorned every surface. There was not a crucifix in sight.

My mom took a seat on the couch and soaked it all in, beaming her approval. "So progressive," she murmured.

I wondered if Ms. Gibson was a Druid.

"Well, Caitlin," Ms. Gibson said, after studying my file for a few minutes, "we're very pleased to have someone with your . . ." she hesitated briefly, "leadership skills . . . join the St. Hilda's family."

"Caitlin's always been very *involved* in school," my mom said, rolling her eyes, like I wasn't right there.

I made a note to inform her that maternal eye-rolling has been documented to have a negative impact on the self-esteem of adolescent girls. I'm sure I can dig up a study somewhere to back this up.

Ms. Gibson gave me a warm smile. "That's wonderful. We have several extracurriculars that could be a nice fit for a girl with your strengths. Have you ever tried Key Club—" She broke off as she noticed my mom frantically signaling ix-nay with her hands.

Like I wasn't *right there*.

"Yes," I answered smoothly, ignoring my flailing parent, "I was in Key Club last year and the year before. I found some startling inefficiencies in their outreach programs and was able to introduce an extensive slate of modernizations. I'd be happy to apply my experience here."

I mean, so what if Mr. Hanson had begged me to pick a different extracurricular for junior year? Even he admitted my improvements were inspired. (No need to dwell on who he claimed they were inspired *by*.)

Club moderators have such nervous dispositions.

"Certainly," Ms. Gibson said, not sounding certain at all. "Now, let's take a moment to discuss your classes."

It was a short discussion. My classes are mostly the same as they would have been back home, the main difference being I don't have to take religion class. My grandma would not approve.

"Well, that's that." Ms. Gibson closed my file and set it on the coffee table. Glancing over my shoulder, she smiled and asked, "Would you like to have a look around the campus now?"

"Sure," I agreed, turning to see what she was looking at.

In the doorway stood a tall girl, maybe a year or two older than me, smiling widely.

"This is my daughter, Tess," Ms. Gibson introduced. "She's also going into the eleventh grade, and she'll be happy to give you a tour."

Tess shared her mother's body type and affinity for hiking sandals, but her hair was dark brown and very curly, and her skin was light brown.

"Hi." She studied me with friendly hazel eyes. "Welcome to St. Hilda's."

Ms. Gibson shooed us politely out the door, and my mom and I followed Tess through the outer office into an open breezeway.

"Caitlin, do you want me to stay, or are you okay on your own?" my mom asked. "Matt texted that Finn is asking for me, and I want to get back to him. This is his first day in a new place."

"Isn't it my first day in a new place, too?"

She gave me an exasperated look. "You're not five years old."

Oh, but how would I ever manage without her tender support? "Fine. No problem. I'll just find my way back to the hotel on my own. It's only a strange island in a foreign country. Piece of cake."

"Great." She shoved cab fare in my hand and was out the door before you could say "favoritism."

"Are you really worried about finding your way home?" Tess asked.

Mindful that I was supposed to be projecting confidence and "chill" now, I smiled and lied. "No, I'm used to getting around on my own." Sure. I walk to the end of my street by myself all the time. Call me Magellan.

Tess smiled. "Did your mom say you're staying in West End? I have yoga down there in a bit, so we can share a taxi if you want."

"Thanks," I said, hiding my relief. "That would be great."

"Come on, I'll give you the deluxe tour. It takes five minutes instead of three." Laughing, she turned and started down the breezeway.

It didn't take the whole five minutes to figure out what she meant. St. Hilda's is much smaller than Our Lady of Perpetual Sorrows. In fact, Tess says there are only about 130 girls in the whole school. She pointed out the preschool and primary school classrooms grouped together on the other side of the office, the middle school on the near side, the small high school building at the end of a short breezeway.

"This is the whole high school?" I asked.

"Well, there are only forty-two girls in grades nine through twelve," Tess explained. "Forty-three now that you're here. We have four regular classrooms, an art room, and a science lab."

"Oh, nice," I said, trying to sound enthusiastic. This place was practically a one-room schoolhouse. I was in *Little House in the Caribbean*. Except even the *Little House on the Prairie* school was co-ed.

Tess looked like she knew what I was thinking. "Yeah, it's small, but it's nice once you get used to it. The student/teacher ratio is fantastic."

"It sounds great." I forced some enthusiasm into my voice.

"Besides," she said, waving her arm in a broad gesture that encompassed the athletic field and the stunning panorama beyond, "where else do you get a view like that from math class?"

I had to laugh. "Nowhere I know of."

We stood there for a minute, Tess admiring the view in the scant, hot breeze, while I produced perspiration at an accelerated rate.

"Hey," I said, noticing for the first time that she hadn't shown me the complex of buildings at the other end of the campus, "what's in those?"

"Oh, that's St. Hugh's," she said.

I looked at her blankly.

"The boys' school," she clarified.

The *what*?

Seeing the look on my face, Tess elaborated. "You know . . . boys? Like girls, but with broader shoulders and shorter attention spans?"

"Yes, I know what boys are. I just wasn't expecting to see . . . well, they told me this school was girls-only."

Tess hooted with laughter. And kept hooting. Her jaw gaped wide, her eyes squeezed shut, and her head hinged back on her neck like the lid of a trash can.

I tapped my foot.

"Oh," she gasped, wiping a tear from her eye, "no wonder you looked so worried. Well." She straightened. "The girls school/boys school thing is kind of a technicality. We share the field and the science lab and stuff. If you take pottery, you'll go over there to use the studio. Gym classes are combined, and so are IB classes."

"Ah."

She gave me a wide grin. "So, do you like it better now?"

I absolutely did, but not for the reason Tess imagined. In my opinion, the main benefit of a co-educational setting is the same point adults cite as its greatest drawback: some girls find some boys highly distracting. Believe me, this is a good thing. Every year at Our Lady of Perpetual Sorrows, each class goes on a mandatory, all-day retreat. Boys and girls get shipped to separate venues to prevent any funny business, but without any boys to obsess over, certain girls descend into utter brutality, turning on their peers like sharks in the womb.

The senior retreat is an overnighter. I plan to get meningitis that weekend.

"Thumbs up for boys," I said, meaning it.

"Yeah, well, that's everything. And I need to leave soon or I'll be late for yoga."

Tess used her phone to call a taxi, and we wandered out to the parking lot. While we waited, she told me all about her yoga instructor and the Outward Bound trip through the Florida Everglades she'd done earlier in the summer.

"I love your dress," I finally interrupted. Mostly so she'd quit describing the "right way" to poo in the swamp, but it was the truth. She wore a drapey black T-shirt dress with a wide neck that snugged up around her hips. A bright square of batik print fabric on the chest gave it tropical pop. It looked stylish and extremely comfy.

"Thanks, it's Tréfle. It's got pock—"

"And that's a very *interesting* outfit you've got on," said a new voice.

I squeaked in surprise. Tess talks kind of . . . loud . . . so I hadn't heard anyone approach. I turned and found two girls about our age standing just behind us. They were *gorgeous*, and one of them was staring at me like I'd stolen her sandwich. And spit in it.

"Thank you," I said, ignoring the dig at my outfit. I'm kind of an expert at ignoring insults. I've had lots of practice.

Both girls gave a small sneer, which unfortunately did nothing to detract from their stunning perfection. Theirs was nothing like Shelby's fresh-faced Free People beauty; these were cover girls come to life, all perfectly shaped brows and dramatic contouring, flawless dark brown skin and perfectly coiffed hair—the kind of girls you see doing eye makeup tutorials on Instagram.

"That's Onessa and that's Viv," Tess said. Her tone was casual, but she seemed a little tense. "They're both in our grade. Say hi to Caitlin, you two."

Onessa and Viv stared down at me, unimpressed.

I gave them a little finger wave. "Delighted to make your acquaintance."

Yes, I said that. Kill me now. This is the humiliation that Shelby's *Downton Abbey* obsession hath wrought.

Onessa and Viv's exquisite eyebrows shot up, and they shared a look.

Just then, a van pulled into the parking lot, and Tess grabbed my hand. "Oh, look, there's our taxi. Gotta run. Byeee!" she called, all but heaving me through the sliding door.

"Farewell," I added.

Oh dear lord.

"You shouldn't worry about Onessa and Viv," Tess said as the taxi bumped along the winding road to West End. "They can be really nice. That back there had nothing to do with you."

"Uh-huh," I said. Forgive me if I sounded skeptical.

"I've known them forever. They're mostly fine. It's just Onessa has been a little difficult," Tess paused, looking thoughtful, "lately."

Yeah, I'm familiar with "difficult" girls. Back at OLPS, Nicky Boucher and Bea Bustamonte are the living embodiments of difficult, existing only to crush the unwary beneath the soles of their penny loafers.

But in a school as small as this one, avoiding difficult personalities will be completely impossible.

The Pickled Pirate
11:43 a.m., August 13

We've been at The Pickled Pirate for three days now. That's a long time to be at The Pickled Pirate.

The guy my parents bought the sailboat from—the sailboat on which we are supposed to *live*—was scheduled to show up with it the morning after we got here. So far? No sign of him.

My mom said not to worry about this because "we're running on Island Time." At which point I merely observed that Island Time seems to be running about three days behind. Now, I ask you, where is the lie? Her reaction was totally uncalled for. I mean, excuse me, but I have already given her all the breaks and I *am* loosened up. As loose as circumstances allow, anyway.

Don't get me wrong, The Pickled Pirate is charming. I'm getting used to the chickens in the yard, and the restaurant serves really good food. The hotel rooms are set back by the gravel road, which makes them kind of dusty, but the walls are painted a very original shade of purple.

See, I'm totally being positive about the experience.

I mostly hang out in the restaurant, which is right on the water. In fact, most customers (of whom there are far fewer than you would expect, given the quality of the nachos) come by dinghy instead of car. By nightfall, the bulkhead dock usually has a small row of bobbing rubber boats tied to it, and if you look down into the water, you can see huge fish feeding on schools of little fish in the light of the restaurant.

At first glance, I thought the big fish were barracuda, but when I went out there with my *Guide to Aquatic Life in the Eastern Caribbean* and a flashlight, I accurately identified them as tarpon. This discovery came as a tarpon-sized relief, because the idea of there being that many huge, hungry barracuda in residence was really dampening my enthusiasm for all of this gorgeous water.

According to the bartender, Bertrand, The Pickled Pirate is very popular with both locals and tourists. I have to take his word for the last part, though, because I haven't seen any tourists—excluding us, that is. And we don't count because we're more like temporary residents.

This lack of tourists extends beyond The Pickled Pirate. I haven't seen tourists at any of the other places we've been over the last few days, either. Not at the beach, or the grocery store, or the T-shirt shops. Nowhere.

You see, it turns out August is not the greatest month to go to the Caribbean. For one thing, it's hot. I mean, yeah, I know, the tropics are *supposed* to be hot, but August is a watch-your-flip-flops-melt-to-the-dock kind of hot. The air is heavy with salt and ozone and, as of yesterday, there is not even a *hint* of breeze. Seriously, it's like someone flipped a switch and shut off the trade winds. I've spent the past three days covered in a thick, slimy layer of sweat, Off!, and sunscreen.

Also, as it turns out, the BVI doesn't have a whole lot going on in August. Because tourism drops off during these months, many of the resorts and restaurants close from the end of July until October. That's why we are currently staying at The Pickled Pirate and not, say, someplace *without* chickens in the yard.

And the reason for all of this: the hot weather, the resort closings, the reduced tourism? It's this little thing Jim Cantore likes to call Hurricane Season.

Yes, that's right, my parents moved their two vulnerable children to the *Caribbean* at the peak of *Hurricane Season*. To live on a *sailboat*.

Yeah. That thing people say about doctors not having any common sense? True. Every word of it.

The Pickled Pirate
4:11 p.m., August 14

Our boat *still* isn't here, but at least I'm not the only one concerned about this anymore. My dad spent the morning on the phone with our yacht broker back in Annapolis while my mom took a taxi into Road Town to see if she could track down the local agent.

I guess his "Island Time" is up.

As for Finn and me, we've fallen into a "Waiting for the Boat" routine. Every morning we get up, have waffles at the bar, and head off to the beach. I'm slowly getting used to this going-off-on-my-own stuff. The BVI is super safe—almost no crime at all—and if I get lost, there are always plenty of friendly people around to offer directions. And it's pretty hard to get lost when traveling from one place to another consists of getting into a taxi, telling the driver where you want to go, and paying him once you get there. Even I can manage that.

I would normally object to having to watch Finn so much, but I think it's important that I pitch in during this difficult time. Plus, my dad is paying me twenty bucks a day—plus expenses—to lie on a beach with a book and, every hour, reapply sunscreen to a squirmy, toothy little boy.

The beach Finn and I like best is called Apple Bay. Finn likes it because it has a wide, sandy beach—some of them are too rocky for sandcastles—and lots of shallow water to play in. I like it because it has shady trees to sit under and because there are a bunch of hot surfer guys who hang out at the other end. I can tell they're surfer guys because they have surfboards, which they sometimes paddle out into the ocean and lie on top of. I'm sure they would surf on top of them, too, if there were any waves.

I guess August in the Caribbean isn't great for surf, either.

Mostly, these guys hang out on the beach a lot, kicking a soccer ball around and swimming. From afar, they kind of look like extras from *Teen Beach Movie*, without the 1960s bathing suits and big musical numbers. I mean, so far. The *Teen Beach* movies were Shelby's favorites the summer of fifth grade so, should these guys happen to break into a spontaneous rendition of "Surf Crazy" and need an extra backup dancer, I can join right in. Then they will accept me as one of their own and we can all hang out together at Big Momma's doing cool-kid stuff.

Hey, a girl can dream.

Of course, dreaming is all I will ever do, especially given the sun-protective clothing I'm forced to wear in order to sit on the beach all day without dying of skin cancer before college. Most people aren't surprised that Finn burns easily—he's a redhead, after all—but blondes can usually handle a little sun. Not me. I was so pale in sixth grade that Afton Hui started calling me the White Walker.

Well, I'm still pale (and Afton Hui is still a jerk) but I'm not ice-zombie-pale. At least, I don't think I am. Shelby doesn't have HBO, so we haven't seen *Game of Thrones*.

My sunproof outfit consists of a lightweight, long-sleeved white shirt and pants from the same UPF 50 material. Finn has a matching set, so together we look like vacationing hazmat workers.

Or possibly just gigantic losers.

Not exactly the kind of ensemble likely to lure hot surfer guys to my end of the beach.

The downside to spending every day reading on the beach is that I have burned through every single book I brought with me, and a visit to the bookstore in Road Town requires a thirty-dollar roundtrip taxi ride. I wonder if Old Fox Books delivers to the BVI.

I also need to talk to Shelby. I promised her I'd call when I got here, but my dad says any roaming charges will come straight out of my allowance, so she's going to have to wait until I find some Wi-Fi.

CHAPTER 5

The Pickled Pirate
9:03 a.m., August 15

It's here!

When I woke up this morning and walked out to the bar for breakfast, Bertrand pointed to a sailboat moored near The Pickled Pirate and said, "There's your boat there, dear."

I ran to a window and, sure enough, a boat I recognized from the listing photos had appeared in the mooring field. I turned to Bertrand to ask about the delivery crew when a booming voice called out, "Hey! Did he say that's *your* boat?"

I recoiled as an enraged white man in a sleeveless T-shirt and board shorts thundered across the floor. The shirt proclaimed that the beatings would continue until morale improved, and the board shorts drooped alarmingly. His skin, apart from a pale, sunglasses-shaped area around his eyes, was a shade I normally associated with strawberry daiquiris and raw tuna.

"Excuse me?" I squeaked in alarm.

He lurched to a halt by the end of the bar and slapped a hand on the top. "It's on my Boaty Ball," he seethed.

Bertrand rolled his eyes and muttered, "Here we go."

"Excuse me?" I asked again.

Lobster-tan man jabbed at his chest with an emphatic finger. "*My* Boaty Ball."

I shook my head, baffled.

Somehow, the man's flesh turned even redder. "I reserved it online! I paid for it! On the app! It's MY BOATY BALL!"

I glanced at Bertrand, who was still indulging in the longest eye-roll in history.

"Look! I'll show you." With a flourish, the man extracted his phone from the front of his board shorts, a move I desperately wish I could unsee. He poked furiously at the screen for a few seconds, then looked up at Bertrand. "Don't you have Wi-Fi in this place?"

Bertrand pointed at a sign by the bar that read "No Wi-Fi. Move along with your foolishness."

"Errrr," the man growled. "Well, I'm telling you, that is *my* Boaty Ball." He stabbed his finger in my direction. "I'm reporting you to customer service. You'll see! IT'S MY BOATY BALL!"

Then he left.

I stared after him. "What was *that*?"

Bertrand grumbled something about "credit card captains" then pulled out his phone and started scrolling through photos of his kids, who are back in St. Vincent and he hasn't seen since New Year's. I poured us both some coffee.

So that was auspicious.

I'll admit, at first I wasn't so into the whole "live-aboard" program, but that was before I contemplated permanent residency at The Pickled Pirate. Now I am a live-aboard *enthusiast*.

We never did get to meet the local yacht agent, which is highly irregular. I would have at least liked to do a walk-through, just to make sure everything is in the condition represented by the listing, but my mom says to have a little faith in my fellow humans.

My dad says I should be thankful there is a boat here at all.

The Pickled Pirate
Hiding under the bar
11:38 a.m., August 15

Well, I hate to say, "I told them so," but . . . I *told* them so!
I suppose our boat's sudden appearance caught everyone
by surprise—*I'd* certainly given up on ever seeing it—so it took us
a while to organize an exploratory expedition. First, there was the
problem of how to get out to it. The delivery crew—whoever they
were—had kindly left it on the Boaty Ball mooring closest to The
Pickled Pirate, but it's not like we could swim out to it. Finn is only
five. And my dad, who has a habit of munching on gummy bears all
day in lieu of a nutritious lunch, has a serious case of gummy gut.
And The Pickled Pirate, though it offers many fine amenities, does
not boast one of those wall-mounted defibrillator kits. So it started
to seem like we'd have to do more waiting around until someone
turned up to give us a ride.

Then Bertrand came to the rescue.

"That's your dinghy over there," he said, waving a bar mop in the
direction of the dinghy dock.

And sure enough, one lonely dinghy sat tied to the bull rail.

"How do you know it's ours?" my dad asked.

Bertrand shrugged. "There's no one else here."

Well, no, not at nine-thirty in the morning. The Pickled Pirate doesn't have much of a breakfast crowd in August. Just us,
actually.

We went over to the dock to have a look.

The dinghy in question was a rigid-bottomed inflatable, about
ten feet long with gray tubes and a little nine-horsepower outboard
engine. A pretty common setup—at least among those who patron-
ize The Pickled Pirate. In fact, there was nothing to distinguish our

dinghy from a million other dinghies in the BVI, other than the eight inches of oily water sloshing around in the bottom. All the other dinghies I've seen at the dock do a pretty good job of keeping the water *outside* of the boat.

"Must have rained last night," my dad mused.

It did not rain last night. It was a sign.

My dad hopped in the dinghy to "run the water out," leaving the rest of us to get ready. My mom, Finn, and I headed back to our adjoining hotel rooms.

"Have you seen my incense kit?" my mom asked.

"Erica, no," I begged. She'd discovered the incense kit in a gift shop in Road Town called Little Denmark. It's the kind of place that carries everything from jewelry and guavaberry liqueur to fishing nets and (unfortunately) Druid paraphernalia. The single time she'd burned her new incense, I'd sneezed for hours. My nose dripped like a Slurpee machine and my eyes looked like swollen stoplights. It was not an experience I cared to repeat.

"The book I'm reading suggests cleansing new spaces with sage," she said, digging through her giant mom-purse. She wouldn't find it in there. I'd stashed it in the minifridge in her hotel room in hopes of containing the smell. "We should prepare the boat to accept our presence."

Shaking my head, I pulled the title and cruising license from my dad's briefcase and stuck them in a special waterproof envelope I'd bought at the marine supply store before we left Annapolis. Then I made Finn put on his life jacket (although, based on my understanding of medieval witch-trial protocols, I'm pretty sure he'd float if he fell overboard) and a hat. I'd have made him put on shoes, too, but Finn has decided shoes are no longer part of his lifestyle. His SpongeBob sneakers were last spotted in five feet of water off the end of the dinghy dock.

I think my parents are heinously irresponsible to let him wander around barefoot, what with the chickens and all, but my mom says he *probably* got a tetanus booster at his last checkup.

Well, that's reassuring. If Finn gets lockjaw, I'm calling Grandma.

My dad retuned to the dock just as my mom finished storing another of her Little Denmark finds, a "ceremonial" whisk broom (I'm pretty sure it's a regular broom that's missing its dustpan) in a Ziploc, so we all hopped in the dinghy and zoomed off to see our new home.

Well, okay, we didn't *zoom*, exactly. The dinghy had seemed zippy enough with my dad in it, but nine-horsepower engines don't push families of four around at much more than a resigned *putt*. We were all in a good mood, though, so we putted along cheerfully, eager and full of hope.

"Look at that, Finn," my dad said, pointing at our boat, "can you tell me what kind of boat it is?"

"Sloop! A'cause it's only got one mast!" Finn, sitting on one of the inflatable tubes that make up the sides of the dinghy, bounced up and down so energetically, I thought he might bounce over the side. (And then wouldn't they all be glad I'd remembered his life jacket?)

"That's right," my dad praised, manning the tiller-drive outboard engine with the air of Russell Crowe at the helm of HMS *Surprise*. Matt Davies, Master and Commander.

"Wow, it's bigger than I expected," I said, bouncing a little myself.

"Forty-five feet is a lot of sailboat," my dad agreed. "We really lucked out, getting such a good price."

Seriously. A boat of this size would usually cost a fortune. My parents had gotten a super good deal on this one, though, because the former owner had been in a big rush to sell.

"This is awesome," I exclaimed.

Hey, I've been at The Pickled Pirate for the better part of a week. That's *plenty* of time to soak up all the pickled, piratical charm. Unless a new strain of chicken evolves, a strain with fins and gills, I am more than ready for life as a live-aboard. The ocean shall be my chicken moat.

"Just think, kids. In a minute or two, we'll be climbing aboard our new home," my dad announced.

"Let's go a little faster," my mom urged, her voice tinged with anticipation.

"Erica, this is as fast as it'll go with all of us in it."

"We're not talking four adults here. Finn weighs forty pounds. Shouldn't it go a *little* faster?"

"Look. I'll show you."

My dad twisted the throttle, opening the engine up wide. From the engine casing came a loud, high-pitched "EHHHHHHHH," but the dinghy maintained its sedate chug. My dad throttled back.

"Well, what if we shift some weight forward? Do you think we could get it up on a plane if Caitlin and I sat in the bow?"

"No, I think the bow would sink. Erica, it's just a dippy little—"

"Holy crab," I breathed (but, instead of crab, I accidentally used a word I wouldn't want my grandma to read.)

"Caitlin. Not in front of your broth—" She caught sight of my face and followed my gaze. "Holy crab," she repeated.

"Oh my god," said my dad.

Because the whole time they'd been bickering over the engine, we'd been motoring (slowly) toward our new home, and now we were close enough to have a pretty good view of it. And by "pretty good" I mean that we could see it clearly, not that it looked any measure of good. In fact, it looked like the opening shot from an episode of *I Shouldn't Be Alive*.

"Ghost ship," Finn breathed reverently.

My mom's eyes were so wide, I thought her eyeballs would fall out.

"Duck," said my dad (or something like that).

"Is it a ghost ship, Erica?" Finn asked. "Will there be dead people?"

"It's not a ghost ship," I told him with conviction. The dead people were still in question.

We were all quiet as my dad steered us on a slow lap around the boat. It was easy to see why Finn's brain had jumped straight to ghost ship. Everything looked ragged and derelict. There were no bright nylon dock lines, no crisp white sails, no shiny teak trimboards. Rust stains ringed the stainless-steel portholes, and the bare, boomless mast stuck up out of the middle of the boat like a toothpick in an olive.

Above the waterline, I saw several large, ugly gouges in the gray fiberglass of the hull. Below the waterline—well, there was no way to know what was going on below the waterline, as every visible inch was covered with slimy, green growth. Long strands of algae trailed like tentacles in the current, and here and there, clusters of barnacles peeked through the grunge.

"Monsters!" cried Finn, delighted.

"Complete monsters," I agreed, looking pointedly at my parents. It's amazing. They'll let just about anybody have kids.

"I thought the hull was supposed to be white," my mom said faintly.

"It was," my dad said, sounding hoarse. "It is."

"So that's . . . that's . . . dirt?" she said, her voice shrill with disbelief.

My dad rubbed his hand over his face. "Yep."

Up on the bow, no anchor dangled before the windlass, and the boat was tied to the pennant of the mooring ball with a thin, red-and-white checkered line that I recognized from a lifetime of miserable gym classes. That's right: our boat was secured with a *jump rope*.

And it only got worse. We motored around to the back of the boat and piled onto the wide stern platform to climb aboard. It was then I finally noticed the boat's name, stenciled in badly faded letters across the hull: *Island Time*.

Fabulous.

We cautiously clambered across the deck, through the sandy cockpit, and down the creaky companionway ladder into the cabin, where we lost the will to go on. Speechless with horror, we stared about the main salon, which in this case is a very grand name for the cramped combination living/dining room, but most things on boats have fancy nautical names. For example, the main salon is lined with built-in cabinets, known as "lockers," two built-in couches ("settees"), and a built-in table ("table") that folds down from the wall. And I wouldn't have touched any of it without a Tyvek suit and a year's supply of Fabuloso (the purple kind, not that weak green stuff).

The upholstery on the settees was faded, stained, and worn through in several places. The finish on the teak paneling was flaking and scratched, and someone had carved a bad word into one of the locker doors. And everything was very, very dirty. Grimy and covered in trash. Home sweet home.

"What is that *smell*?" I asked, taking shallow breaths.

My mom must have popped an emergency positivity pill because, after a long moment, she recovered enough to chirp, "Look, all of this is cosmetic. With a little elbow grease, this will be lovely. What a great opportunity to put our own shine on this boat and give it new life!"

My dad listened expressionlessly to this little pep talk. I snorted in disbelief. Finn pulled a Goldfish cracker from his pocket and tossed it in his mouth.

I handed my mom her smudge stick and Ziploc baggie, which I'd been holding for her while she held on to Finn. "You're gonna need a bigger whisk broom."

Her mouth was smiling but her eyes were stabbing as she told me, with notably less sunshine in her voice, "This is going to be a wonderful project for us to work on as a family."

"Are you kidding me right now?" I asked incredulously. "This isn't *Captain Ron*. We're not in some zany but ultimately heart-warming comedy, Kurt Russell is not coming to save us, and *that couch*"—I pointed at the portside settee, which had a stain on it that still looked wet—"probably has cholera!"

Truly, I preferred stressed workaholic Erica to this new, delusionally optimistic version. If we were about to be eaten by sharks—which was starting to seem like a real possibility given that our new home is a shipwreck waiting to happen—she'd probably be like, "Oh, what a wonderful opportunity to merge with the life force of these majestic creatures!"

Then she got a look at the kitchen (or "galley" as those of us who are unwilling victims of our parents' midlife crises must learn to call it.)

"Matt? Sweetheart?" she said. I detected a desperate edge to her cheery tone. "Where is the stove?"

We all stared into the galley. In place of the shiny, stainless-steel range shown in the listing photos was a grimy Igloo cooler. The cooler had been left open (which was a considerate thing to do, really, because closed coolers can go super funky) and was overflowing with empty beer bottles. Carib and Heineken, I noted.

My dad's always telling me that, when I grow up, I should steer clear of guys who drink imported beer. Now I get why.

"How are we supposed to cook without a stove?" my mom said. Her voice had gone a bit wavery.

My dad looked nervous. "Umm . . . I saw a grill on deck."

"A grill?" Her voice started to rise. "How are we supposed to feed this family for a year with a *grill*?!"

She glanced at me, closed her mouth, and launched into her breathing exercises. I watched with interest. Considering everything wrong with our current situation, a missing stove would not have been the thing that sent *me* over the edge, but I guess squalor seems like a much bigger deal when there's no burner on which to brew your herbal tea.

"Cooool," Finn crooned, emerging from the nearest locker with a half-full box of cigars and a flare gun.

"Uh, why don't you let me have that, buddy," my dad said.

"No!" Finn clutched his treasures to his chest and bared his pearly little teeth.

Not wanting to get bitten in the crossfire, I wandered toward the back of the boat ("aft") and opened the narrow door. Inside was a sleeping cabin with a large bed and an attached bathroom ("head"). My parents' cabin.

I closed the door, turned, and walked forward, squeezing past my family.

There were two narrow doors in the front of the boat. I opened the one on the left and found myself in a tiny cabin with a set of built-in bunk beds, a built-in dresser, and a small hanging locker. Across from the bunks was another door, which led to a small head.

I backed out of the cabin and opened the door on the right. It led to a head that looked suspiciously like the one I'd seen two seconds before.

Leaving the door on the right open, I went back through the door on the left, opened the door to the attached head—and found myself staring through the head, out the door I'd left open, and into the main salon.

I turned back to the doorways and shook my head. No, it couldn't be. They wouldn't do this to me. I scanned the cabin, desperately searching for some other door I might have overlooked.

Nothing.

"Matt? Erica?" I called, breathing a little quickly. "Where is the third cabin?"

CHAPTER 6

The Pickled Pirate
At the bar, burying my sorrows in nachos and a (virgin) banana
daiquiri
7:34 p.m., August 15

When we got back to The Pickled Pirate, I went straight to my room and gave my flip-flops a blast with the complimentary hair dryer. Flip-flop funk is a particularly vile form of stench, and they'd been submerged in oily seawater the whole ride back to shore. Because, although my dad had *just* run the water out of it not an hour before, the dinghy was once more awash with several inches of water.

Funny I hadn't noticed it raining. Again.

Once my flip-flops were dry, I joined my parents, who were at the bar consulting with Bertrand. According to Bertrand, the *Island Time* was already moored at seven-thirty this morning when he arrived at work, and he'd seen no sign of the yacht broker or the delivery crew.

My dad used his phone (without even a mention of exorbitant roaming charges) to call our yacht broker back in Annapolis and sent him several photos he'd snapped of the *Island Time*'s deck and cabin. The good news was that our broker hadn't forwarded my dad's check to the seller yet. The bad news was the seller and *his* broker had both mysteriously disappeared, so our broker couldn't get our three-thousand-dollar deposit back. *But*, he said, on the bright side, we now own a forty-five-foot sailboat for only three thousand dollars.

Parental morale launched like a rocket at that news. They giggled and kissed and said something about spending Valentine's Day in Mustique. It was revolting. And it fell to me to deliver the reality check.

I don't want to sound like a spoiled little brat, but when they first announced this scheme, my parents promised—promised!—that I would have my own cabin. I cannot share a room with my *five-year-old* brother. Even if he were like other people's five-year-old brothers—you know, *not* evil incarnate—I wouldn't want to share a cabin with him. Five-year-olds go to bed at, like, eight o'clock.

But Finn is not like other five-year-olds. He bites. He designs elaborate booby traps. He walks in on me when I'm naked.

Not my ideal roommate.

And I don't care *how* many sad looks they give me, I am not going back out to that stinky, disgusting boat. I will just live out the next year here at The Pickled Pirate with Bertrand and the chickens.

"Caitlin, don't be silly," my mom said. "We didn't lie. We *thought* there were three cabins. The literature *said* there were three cabins. We'll just have to make the best of it."

"*We?* Oh, I'm sorry. Are *you* going to be sharing a cabin with the five-year-old hell spawn, then?"

"I know it's going to be quite an adjustment—"

"No," I interrupted. "Living in the Caribbean is going to be quite an adjustment. Going to an all-girls school is going to be quite an adjustment. Sharing a room with Finn is just plain. Not. Happening."

"Well, where exactly do you think everyone should sleep then, Miss Persnickety?"

My dad gave me this obnoxious nickname when I was about Finn's age, and I react to it as well now as I did then.

"How about back in *Annapolis*," I screamed, "where we *belong*!"

The Pickled Pirate
9:30 p.m., August 15

I will be sharing a cabin with Finn. I will have no privacy, and I'll probably have some new scars to show for it, but for seventy-five dollars a week, I'll cope.

Seventy-five dollars being the figure my dad and I agreed upon for my weekly allowance if I will share the forward cabin with Finn. Cheerfully.

"Because it's still cheaper than a bigger boat or a divorce," he said.

I know I should feel guilty, but with that kind of income, I could eventually save up enough to commission a Cameo video by my greatest hero, Fiona Hill. Besides, I think I'm going to need the extra money. I bought a can of Coke from Thelma's Market this afternoon, and it cost me three dollars and fifty cents!

The Pickled Pirate
Sitting on the dinghy dock
10:24 a.m., August 16

This morning I awoke ready to spearhead the cleaning of *Island Time*, which will require vast quantities of Pine-Sol and probably borax. And gloves, and sponges, and scrub brushes . . . I was making a list when I got a call from Shelby.

I knew what she was going to say, and I didn't want to hear it, much less pay roaming charges for the privilege. I'd hoped to head off this call with an email, but I had far too much to report to type it all out on my phone, and my dad wouldn't let me use his laptop because he "has a book to write." (Right. I'm sure the world is hotly anticipating the release of his treatise on oozy tropical diseases.) But I had delayed too long and now I owed her this call, no matter the cost. This was my penance. And, with my new allowance, I supposed I could afford it. I took a deep breath and tapped Accept.

"About time!" she squealed, before launching into a ten-minute description of all the cute/horrible things her little junior sailing campers had been up to, Carson the Tech Crew Boy's attempts to master his new Onewheel, and all the shows she's started watching. I'm a little peeved she started *Heartstopper* without me because that was next on *our* watchlist, but I guess I can't expect her to wait a whole year for me. That would be selfish and unreasonable, and I'm a reasonable person.

I would do it for her is all I'm saying.

"So how's our project going?"

Quite obviously, I have not made much progress on Operation: Not a Freak. Between acclimating to my new surroundings and visiting St. Hilda's and waiting for our boat to arrive and fighting off the chickens and, you know, jet lag . . . well, there just hasn't been time. Believe me, I'm keen on the idea of becoming a new Caitlin. A better Caitlin. A more relaxed, less socially awkward Caitlin. Away from Shelby, though, it just doesn't seem likely to happen. If she'll just look at this realistically, she'll see that the most probable outcome of any such attempt would be me making the exact same fool of myself, only in front of an entirely new population of people. And who actively pursues public humiliation when there are forty-five-foot sailboats out there *begging* to be cleaned and organized?

I explained all this Shelby, who was not in the mood for reality.

"You do not clean for fun anymore," she ordered.

What? "I did not agree to that!"

"The New Caitlin would rather go to the beach. Have you even *been* to the beach yet?"

"Only every day," I informed her.

"Really?" She sounded surprised.

"Really," I said proudly.

"Are you sunburned?"

"Nope."

"Why not?"

"Why not what?"

"You sunburn in Annapolis in February. If you've been to the beach in the Caribbean every day, you should be charbroiled by now."

"Um. I've been really careful?"

"Ah-ha! I knew it! You've been wearing your Freak Suit, haven't you?"

The Freak Suit is what Shelby calls my sun-repellant beach attire.

"Would I do that?" I asked. Not a lie—an *evasion*.

"Did anyone see you? Please tell me no one saw you."

"Oh. Well, it depends," I hedged. "Do you mean 'noticed' saw, or just 'laid eyes on' saw?"

At this point, Shelby did about three dollars' worth of wailing and gnashing of teeth before she got ahold of herself. "Look, no more, okay? From now on, you wear the yellow bikini."

Oh, my. The yellow bikini. My feelings for the yellow bikini are really complicated. It exposes basically everything to the sun, which is just begging for melanoma, but it has a nice little layer of strategic padding sewn into the top, which even I will admit looks quite fetching.

But, I mean, what if someone realizes the top is all padding? Then I'll be known as the boobless girl who's trying to hide her booblessness. That's ten times worse than owning your booblessness. And I just don't know if that padding makes up for the lack of coverage. Skin cancer is no joke. Plus, my butt is on the scrawny side. That is not my insecurities talking; this fact has been verified by independent observers. Last month, Shelby and I were standing outside the mall waiting for her mom to pick us up when some guys in a red Corolla cruised by. Shelby was all excited and whispering, "Yay! They think we're hot! They're checking us out!" Then one of the guys stuck his head out the window and shouted at me, "Hey! You ain't got no a—" Well, never mind his exact words. He expressed that he did not find me callipygous.

I hate the mall.

Anyway, with little to hold it in place, the skimpy yellow bikini bottoms tend to creep up on me. Way up. You know what I mean. And that's an uncomfortable place to be sunburned.

"But I'll get burned!" I protested.

"Sit in the shade," she said heartlessly, "and don't you dare wrap yourself in a towel."

In the end, just to get her off the phone before I exhausted my current funds and had to sell plasma to pay my T-Mobile bill, I promised Shelby I'd wear the cursed bikini next time I go to the beach.

This, of course, means that I can never again go to the beach. Oh well, I'm sure there are lots of other things to do in the Virgin Islands. Right?

The Pickled Pirate
5:15 p.m., August 16

I was serious about never going to the beach again—I even planned to hold a symbolic burning of the Freak Suit, just so I wouldn't be tempted—but that was before Finn's monster meltdown this morning.

He brought it on himself. A dock is a stupid place to play with tiny plastic toys, a point my dad unintentionally demonstrated by running Finn's SpongeBob LEGO set over with a dock cart. The Krusty Krab was instantly reduced to primary-colored shrapnel. A few pieces were pecked up by chickens and the rest flew off the dinghy dock and sank.

Now, if it had been *my* LEGO blocks whizzing all over paradise, my parents would have lectured me to be more careful with my belongings, exercise some situational awareness, blah blah blah. But was Finn subjected to a tiresome homily on personal responsibility?

Spoiler: no, he was not.

In fact, Finn got no lecture at all. Not even the one I've been getting pretty regularly about Island Time and "rolling with the punches" and "the value of patience." (And yes, patience applies here. Think about it: any LEGO that goes into a chicken will come out of that chicken eventually.) No, what Finn got instead was coddling and hugs and an organized rescue mission.

So typical. I get preachy clichés; Finn gets whatever he's screaming about. My mom even put on her snorkeling stuff and started free diving for tiny blocks. Maybe I'd get more respect if I acted like Finn. It seems there's something highly motivating about the occasional ankle chomp.

Overall, my mom did a pretty good job LEGO hunting. Sunken LEGO are not the easiest things in the world to retrieve. Not only do they bury themselves in the sand on impact, their bright colors are notably less vivid in five feet of water. And my mom's expertise in rectal foreign body retrieval hardly qualifies her to be the next Bob Ballard. But she found enough pieces to mostly reconstruct the restaurant, although Squidward and the dumpster remained missing. Finn, still sniffling, examined our efforts with suspicion.

My dad sidled over and shoved a twenty in my palm. "Take him to the beach," he murmured.

"Can't."

"Bull."

"No, really, Matt. I can't do the beach anymore."

This is where most fathers would say: "What's wrong, honey? Did something happen at the beach? I don't want you to do anything that makes you uncomfortable."

Not my dad.

"Either you take him to the beach or you spend the afternoon squeezing the missing LEGOs out of those chickens. Your choice."

So off we went, Finn in his Freak Suit and me in a T-shirt and shorts. Yes, the yellow bikini was underneath. As promised, I shucked my top layer as soon as we got to Apple Bay. And, with Shelby's pep talk fresh in my mind, I walked right past our usual spot in front of the restaurant and headed straight for the far end of the beach—the end where all the surfers hang out.

Not that I walked right up to them or anything. I mean, it's a really wide beach, and they were all in the water, anyway. I did stake out a spot in their general vicinity, though.

I laid out my towel in the shade of a short, wide-leafed tree and did my best to look like someone with a manageable number of insecurities. Which was no freaking walk in the park, okay? Seriously, to set myself up for that level of scrutiny my first time out in the yellow bikini? That's big-hearted bravery, that's what it is. Maybe not brave like Benjamin Bratt's character in *The Great Raid*, rescuing all those American POWs from the Cabanatuan death camps and carrying them back to allied territory on foot. More like Taylor Swift pledging to fly commercial sometimes. Brave like that.

I probably should have worn the yellow bikini in front of Shelby and my parents a few times before trying it out in the real world. A couple of practice runs might have desensitized me to the way it showcases my pasty skin and bony shoulders. I tried hard not to think of the single time I'd worn a tank top on Out-of-Uniform Day. Nicky Boucher told everyone I looked like a war orphan. But I've been doing some push-ups lately, trying to bulk up a little, and it seems to be working. Plus, Shelby assured me that the pale-yellow color and Swiss-dot pattern make me look ethereal (good dead) instead of corpse-like (bad dead.)

I slathered sunscreen on all the places the bikini didn't cover (because, even in the shade, the sun's harmful rays can reflect off of sand and water, causing serious burns) and pulled out a paperback I borrowed from The Pickled Pirate's book swap.

Yeah, I know you're not supposed to "borrow" books from a book swap, but I couldn't bear to leave any of *my* books where someone might take them. Those book swap books look like they've been through hell. They're ripped and faded, and more than a few have that distinctive wave to the pages that means they were dropped in the drink or left out in the rain at some point. Many have torn covers or, in a few pitiful cases, no cover at all.

That will never happen to *my* books. Not while there's breath in my lungs.

The book I borrowed/rescued from the book swap is in relatively good shape, which is to say it still has a cover. In fact, it was the cover that first caught my attention. It says *Rebellious Passion* in gold script and features a man and a woman, their clothes in tatters, embracing on the listing deck of a pirate ship.

Now, I know I mentioned this before, but I have kind of a thing for pirate ships. And pirates. Especially dashing pirates who eschew

buttons on their shirts and are named things like Blade the Buccaneer. Besides, I was dying to find out what happened to these
people's clothes.

By the end of the third chapter, I was well on my way to an answer. The heroine, Persephone, had, unfortunately, "stood helpless
while he split her bodice on his dagger" on page seven, and had torn
her petticoat to dab at the head wound of a fellow captive on page
eighteen. By page thirty-one, with the main characters still at odds,
I was starting to wonder how her clothes were ever going to survive
until the scene depicted on the cover. Despite their instant sense of
connection, she and Blade the Buccaneer were nowhere near the
passionate embrace stage, and she was already cruising around with
her skirt slashed off above her knees and her boobs spilling out of
her chemise.

I paused to add "chemise" to the vocabulary list I've been keeping (you never know when "bourgeoning" will show up on the
SATs) and absently noted the squelch of sand as Finn wandered up
from the water's edge.

"PB&J in the backpack," I said.

"Brilliant. Thanks," said a voice much too deep to belong to any
five-year-old.

My pencil froze mid-word, an outward indication of what my
brain was doing at just that moment.

I took a deep breath and held it. Okay, so . . . that wasn't Finn.
That sounded like a real boy. No, not a boy—a *guy*! Exhaling slowly,
I turned my head and found two tanned feet planted in the sand
beside my towel.

The tanned feet led to tanned legs, which were covered with a
sprinkling of golden hair and a pair of blue board shorts. Above
those was a tanned chest, not covered by anything at all.

Eep.

Now, I've been in the junior sailing program at my yacht club since I was eight, so I am not unaccustomed to bare male chests *or* board shorts. But the bare chests in my previous experience have never been quite so broad. Or so tan. Not that we don't have sun in Annapolis, but sailor boys, unlike surfer boys, wear life jackets most of the time, which makes for some very odd tan lines. Basically, they look like they have pale sweater vests tattooed on their skin. Not really the stuff of daydreams.

But there were no tan lines at all on this particular bare chest. Just lots of smooth skin, and muscles . . .

It was at this point that I realized I was lying on the ground staring at a stranger's chest.

I jerked my gaze up above his neck and met a pair of the brightest blue eyes I've ever seen. Really, magnificently blue. Not blue like the sky or the ocean, or anything trite like that. More like the intense, eye-catching blue of an Ikea warehouse—that blue that says, "Look inside. You know you want to. We have meatballs."

"Hi," I breathed.

"Hi." Those Ikea eyes glittered down at me. I couldn't help but notice they were set in a completely gorgeous face—tanned, of course—topped by golden brows and thick, wavy golden hair.

Wow. And, again: wow.

And those Ikea eyes shone down at me now, focused and expectant, like I was the answer to all his dreams.

Or, oops, was just he waiting for me to answer him?

"What?" I asked dumbly.

"I said," he repeated, "you probably don't want to let your brother eat those green sea grapes. He'll be sick."

"Brother? What broth—oh! Finn!" I shot up, dropping my book in the sand, and scanned the beach for my wayward brother. I spotted him three yards away, picking round, green things off the branches of my shade tree.

"Finn!"

Finn looked over disinterestedly.

"Do not eat those. They'll make you sick."

"Will they make me throw up?"

"Umm . . ." I looked to Ikea Eyes for an answer.

"Yes," he confirmed.

"Good. I like to throw up," Finn said sanguinely (check out that vocab word!) and chomped down on a sea grape.

Behold, my totally normal little brother.

"Finn, cut it out." I walked over and knocked the remaining sea grapes from his hand, then retreated back to my towel as quickly as possible. Partly to get out of biting range, but mostly so I didn't have to stand up for very long in my bikini. I could feel the bottoms staging a northern migration with every step.

I dug a sandwich out of my backpack and tossed it to Finn. "Eat food, not sour grapes." Turning back to Ikea Eyes, I said, "Hey, thank you so much. You saved him."

"No worries." His accent wasn't Caribbean or American, or even some combination of the two, like Tess's. In fact, he sounded just like Hugh Grant in *Love Actually* (Shelby's mom's favorite Christmas movie, which we watch every year). I wondered if he was a tourist from England or if, like Tess's mom, he belonged to the island's ex-pat community.

Ex-pats are people who have permanently moved to another country but have not changed citizenship. The Caribbean is full of them, especially those hailing from cold, gloomy places like England and Pittsburgh.

"Here"—he bent down and pulled my book out of the sand—"you dropped your book." He started to hand it back to me then paused, arrested by the cover. His eyebrows rose and one corner of his mouth tipped up in a little smile.

My stomach lurched like I'd eaten a unripe sea grape.

"Thanks," I said, snatching the book from his hand. I tried to be cool about it, but I could feel my face burning like I'd applied SPF 15 instead of SPF 50.

I mean, kill me now. The snackiest guy I've ever seen walks up *and* talks to me (both of these firsts!) and I'm lying around reading the kind of book where people slice garments off each other while my little brother poisons himself. I wanted to crawl under my towel and suffocate myself in the sand.

Ikea Eyes didn't seem especially perturbed by my taste in literature, however. I mean, maybe he was silently judging me but, if so, fair enough.

"Are you on vacation?" he asked.

Oh my god, he wasn't running away! He was staying! To chat! With ME!

"Uh," I stuttered a little. "No. I mean, not really. Well, maybe like a really, really long vacation, I guess?"

"Oh." He grinned, still giving me that crooked little smile, but now it invited me to laugh with him. "Well, so long as we've got that straight." He offered his hand. "I'm Tristan."

I took his hand automatically. It was warm and covered with the superfine grit of dried salt water. "Caitlin."

He kept hold of my hand as he asked, "So, Caitlin, just how long is your vacation, then?"

"A year."

"A year?" He let go of my hand, which was fortunate because it was growing damp.

Instead of backing off, though, he plopped down in the sand beside my towel and asked, "Will you be going to school here?"

I was suddenly experiencing some kind of tachycardia. My heart beat so rapidly, I worried he could hear it. I planted my sweaty palm on my towel and tried not to pant as I answered, "St. Hilda's, grade eleven."

"Oh, brilliant. My sister's at St. Hilda's, same year."

He pronounced it "Scent Hilda's." Swoon.

When it comes to guys back in Annapolis, I'm pretty good at estimating ages. None of the guys back home look like *this*, however. I could tell Tristan was older—at least a senior, but maybe even old enough to have graduated. And I didn't want to offend him by implying he was still in high school if he wasn't.

Playing it safe, I asked, "How 'bout you?"

"Oh," he gave me a lazy smile, "I was going into twelfth, but I'm taking a year off. Thought I'd give everyone else time to catch up."

My racing heart stuttered. Catch up? Had he skipped a grade? Not only gorgeous, but brilliant, too! Not that you have to be brilliant to skip a grade, as I well know, but Tristan didn't strike me as an ABCya! aficionado. Which left only the option of natural genius.

Could it be that the very first guy to ever willingly talk to me is my soulmate? Could this be happening, just like in *Rebellious Passion* (minus all the bodice-ripping)? Could he be my destiny?

"Wow. That sounds awesome."

Maybe my parents would let me skip school this year and go back next year with my age group. Ha. Fat chance. Not that I'd want to prolong my stay in high school anyway. Or endure a whole senior year without Shelby. But a year of complete abandon, lying on the beach reading pirate romance beside my soulmate, *would* be nice.

"Not too rough," Tristan agreed. "So, where are you staying for the year?"

"Soper's Hole, mostly," I answered, naming the little harbor where the *Island Time* is moored. "We're living on a sailboat. Or we will be, as soon as we move aboard. For now, we're at The Pickled Pirate."

"Really? Well, that is an adventure," he said admiringly. "Here, come and meet the guys. Enzo and Lucas are neighbors of yours, of a sort." He stood and offered me a hand up. "I'll introduce you."

"Uh . . ." I hesitated.

Besides feeling slightly overwhelmed at the prospect of meeting more new people—new *male* people—wearing only my wandering yellow bikini, I have a firm policy against appearing socially with Finn, due to his aforementioned biting and barfing.

And leaving him by himself for any length of time is never an option. Finn *lives* for unsupervised moments.

"Don't be shy; they won't bite." Tristan winked. "Not if you're with me, anyway." Reclaiming my hand, he pulled me to my feet and motioned at Finn. "Come on, little man."

I probably should mention that Finn doesn't like cutesy nicknames. He broke my parents of the habit early, and even our grandma gave it up after he called her a bad word for giving him a reindeer sweater last Christmas.

Now he stared at Tristan through slitty eyes, an all-too-familiar expression on his face. It's his patented Spawn of Satan look. It can mean anything from "I'm going to bite you in the calf" to "I'm going to lock you in an old dog kennel in the basement and leave you for dead." I'm not naïve enough to think that Finn couldn't maim a six-foot-plus teenage male if he really wanted to. The kid's vicious.

I caught Finn's eye. "Ice cream," I mouthed, widening my eyes expressively. "Lots of ice cream."

He studied me a long moment before nodding. Faster than you can say "The Bad Seed," his face relaxed, and he wandered behind us across the hot sand looking so sweet you could pour him over pancakes.

Honestly, I had bigger things to worry about than a vengeful Finn. With every step, I could feel my bikini bottoms inching their way toward my butt crack.

Shelby never covered what to do in the event of an exposed bathing suit wedgie. I don't think it occurred to either of us that I might actually have to *move* while wearing the yellow bikini. I hadn't envisioned doing anything more active than lying daringly on my beach towel, so now I was at a loss. Did good manners dictate I pretend nothing was going on back there and let my cheeks hang out in the sun? Or was I supposed to oh-so-casually reach back and un-floss myself? What if I fixed it and it crept right back up on me? I risked becoming that-girl-who-picks-at-her-butt-all-the-time, which is even worse than being that-scrawny-girl-who-skipped-third-grade. That is probably not what Shelby had in mind when she urged me to reinvent myself.

Surely fashion scientists have come up with a provision for this, a waterproof adhesive or something. If I'm going to live in the Caribbean for a year, I'm going to have to come up with a fix.

Now, at this point, between the migrating bathing suit bottoms, the stunningly handsome escort, and the prospect of meeting a bunch more new people, the old Caitlin would have been paralyzed with social anxiety. The old Caitlin would have feared Tristan was just setting her up to be the butt of some elaborate joke (and she probably would have been right about that). She would have convinced herself that the half-naked guys down the beach would recognize her on sight as a scrawny little geek who loves to organize pantries and visit her grandma. But the old Caitlin is out, and New Caitlin is in. Just as I started to get really worked up, I remembered the only useful advice Shelby had given me that didn't involve concealing my age or swearing off Evernote: fake it till you make it.

So I sallied forth, projecting confidence and sophistication . . . and it worked!

I met all of them. First there was Byron, a guy with slender braids looped up in a man bun who appeared to be dozing on top of his surfboard. He didn't open his eyes when we were introduced, but he waved a hand in my direction. Pretty friendly, I thought, given that we'd interrupted his nap. Enzo and Lucas, the guys Tristan mentioned were "neighbors of a sort," turned out to be twins. Both twins have dark eyes, tan skin, and shortish, straight hair, but Enzo's hair is black while Lucas's is Easter-egg purple. Like Tristan, their accents were English, but they didn't sound nearly as business class.

"And that's Joe," Tristan said offhandedly, gesturing toward a guy just coming out of the water.

Joe set his board down in the sand and came over, dripping wet, to shake my hand. He had a nice face, hair in short twists, dark brown skin, and his chest was nothing to sneeze at, either. Not that I was checking him out—I mean, Tristan is the most gorgeous guy ever and probably my destiny. Joe's abs were, like, right there, though. A less devoted girl would have noticed them is all I'm saying.

Sadly, I was unable to judge the chests of the three other guys, as they were all wearing T-shirts. In fact, Joe shrugged on a ratty old Hi-Ho tee a moment later, and I could only be grateful Tristan hadn't followed his selfish example. Tristan's chest made the world a more beautiful place.

But most amazing of all? Not a single one of these guys looked at me and went, "What is *she* doing here? She shouldn't even be talking to us. This girl is clearly fifteen years old, and I can tell her summer playlist is nothing but Disney classics. And she has the sex appeal of a sea cucumber."

And it gets better.

After we all did the introduction thing, Lucas confirmed that they really are my neighbors. Sort of.

"Our house is on Copper Point," he said simply.

There was no need to say more. The house on Copper Point is known throughout the Virgin Islands. The only house more widely known is Sir Richard Branson's, and that one was on *MTV Cribs*. No noncelebrity house can compete with that.

Copper Point is a prominent cliff just around the island from Soper's Hole, and the twins' house is an architectural marvel of wood and glass that spills down the bluff in five separate levels, connected by outdoor staircases.

The only thing more incredible than that house is the fact Lucas and Enzo are willing to categorize me as a neighbor, just because my family's boat is (barely) floating in the harbor around the corner.

"Jonas is a neighbor, too," Enzo added.

"Jonas?" I asked.

Joe, the dripping guy, opened his mouth to explain when Tristan chimed in, "Caitlin's going to be at St. Hilda's this year."

"Scent Hilda's" again. God, even his accent is hot! Every single word he speaks accentuates his devastating wit and gorgeousness. And I wasn't the only one enraptured. Enzo and Lucas noticed, too. They both stared at him, their mouths slightly agape.

"Well," Enzo said after a pause, "that's some magnificent news!" His brother continued to watch Tristan with an absorbed look on his face. "You'll ride to school with us, then. We're next door at St. Hugh's."

Holy crab. The old Caitlin would never have been asked to carpool with boys. And even if she had, her mother would never have *let* her carpool with boys, because walking saves the planet or whatever.

New Caitlin's mother might not allow it either, actually, but New Caitlin will handle this the same way the old Caitlin did—by catching a ride every day and keeping her mouth shut.

"Oh, sure, thanks," I said, trying to sound casual. New Caitlin was appreciative but not thrilled to pieces by this offer. This kind of thing happened to her all the time.

At this point, Byron the Napper roused and barked, "Lunch!"

The guys decided on a little lunch stand down the road that's built into the trunk of a banyan tree. Finn spotted it several days ago and asked to try it, but so far, I've resisted. I mean, do you know what lives in trees? Bugs. And, around here, lizards. And probably lots of other disgusting stuff that I haven't heard about yet.

"Would you care to join us?" Tristan asked.

"Actually, we brought sandwiches," I explained regretfully. Okay, maybe not *too* regretfully. "But thanks anyway."

Tristan hung back as the others stampeded off down the beach. To *talk* to *me*! I was grateful for my sunglasses because I could feel my eyes turning to emoji hearts. "So," he began, "have you—"

"I want my ice cream now," Finn interrupted.

He'd been unusually good through all of this, playing quietly with a pile of shells a few feet away, but I guess all that talk of lunch had stimulated his appetite. Sea grapes must not be very filling.

Tristan crouched down so he was eye level with Finn. "What do you say you give me a minute with your sister, little man."

Oh my god! Was he going to ask for my number? No one had ever asked for my number before!

I was so excited that I completely missed the second "little man" offense. I only learned about it later, when Finn was attempting to justify what he did next.

"Can I give you a shell first?" Finn asked.

"That's very nice of you," Tristan replied.

Wait, Finn was never nice.

Finn unzipped the webbed pocket on the sleeve of his Freak Suit and gingerly pulled out a large shell, which he dropped onto Tristan's waiting palm.

"Okay, great shell," Tristan commented. "No chips at all. Thank—AHHH!"

He shot up and said a word that made Finn grin.

"What's wrong?" I cried. And I wasn't talking to Tristan. "Tell me right now, you little jerk!"

Finn kept smugly silent.

Tristan had turned his hand upside down and was shaking it forcefully, trying to dislodge the small shell that dangled from the skin of his palm.

Now, there's nothing remarkable about a dangling shell. Shells often dangle . . . from necklaces, or keychains—sometimes even from earrings. But not usually from palms. I leaned forward for a better look. Not unless they're attached by a giant purple claw, viciously clamped onto the fleshy area between the thumb and pointer finger.

Oh dear.

I persuaded the hermit crab to let go by repeatedly tapping its claw with a large rock. It finally dropped to the sand and retreated into its shell.

"Can I see that for a sec?" Tristan eased the rock from my hand and bent over the now harmless-looking shell.

Whack! Whack! Whack!

Finn and I both gasped. And, with that, the crab had pinched its last palm.

Still brandishing the rock, Tristan turned and studied Finn with intent.

Believe me, I empathized, but I couldn't allow it. I felt it was implied in my twenty-dollar Finn-sitting fee that I would not let people bash him with rocks. Instead, I grabbed the neck of Finn's shirt and demanded he apologize.

Which he did. Very sweetly.

Holding his thumb against his palm to staunch the bleeding, Tristan said, "I'm sure it was an accident." But he didn't look sure.

I'm sure it was deliberate. Successfully becoming New Caitlin is clearly going to require ditching the Demon Spawn. For the moment, though, the best I could do was haul Finn away and give Tristan time to recover. And, hopefully, to forget.

Tristan walked me back to the other end of the beach, keeping a wary eye on Finn.

"Have you heard about the Full Moon Party?" he asked.

I hadn't.

"There's one happening tomorrow night. You should come."

Now, I love parties; at least the kind of parties where you swim in a pool, or jump in a bouncy house, or watch the animatronic animals sing between rounds of Whac-A-Mole. But the kind of party I worried Tristan was talking about, the kind people start having once they turn fourteen and suddenly decide there is something fundamentally uncool about Skee-Ball and robotic rats? The kind of parties where there's nothing to do but stand around talking to people who aren't interested in what you have to say and aren't even willing to pretend? The parties where you spend the whole time trying to look like you're not miserable and you have lots of people to talk to even though, in fact, you are and you don't? Those parties are not my cup of tea.

Normally, this would not be a problem for me, because I am not the kind of person who gets invited to those parties.

Unfortunately, Shelby *is* the sort of person who gets invited to parties (not often, thank the blessed mother Mary, but occasionally some guy, dazzled by her artless beauty, forgets that she is not technically "in-crowd"). And, while I hate to speak ill of a friend, Shelby is also the sort of person who insists on dragging her faithful bestie along with her, then abandons said bestie on the loser couch (not the one by the Bagel Bites, the one by the picked-over Costco veggie platter.) So I've been to enough parties to know I don't like them.

But New Caitlin probably *does* enjoy this kind of party (although surely she still enjoys singing rats, too?) And, anyway, a Full Moon Party sounds like it could fall into the former category, the party-with-something-to-do category. Astronomy is awesome.

And I was invited by none other than a gorgeous, Ikea-eyed genius, so how could it not be amazing?

"Why not," I said, projecting coolness and confidence, "I love full moons."

Tristan laughed like that was the funniest thing he'd ever heard. "Brilliant! I'll see you there."

He winked at me as he walked away.

He must feel it, too!

CHAPTER 7

The Pickled Pirate
Locked in the bathroom
8:02 p.m., August 16

My parents totally blew me off when I told them what Finn had done. I'm not surprised, just disappointed. That child lives a consequence-free existence, which is how we find ourselves in our current predicament, the one in which even Catholic school kindergartens hesitate to admit him.

"You can't think he did it on purpose, Caitlin," my mom reasoned. "Hermit crabs back home don't have *claws*. Finn couldn't have known. He was just being friendly."

I don't buy this for a second. Not even a five-year-old could mistake that crustaceous beach monster for the harmless little aquatic hermit crabs we have in Annapolis. Even if he failed to process the fact that this hermit crab obviously lived on *land*, the giant claw hanging out of the shell like a prickly purple "Do Not Disturb" sign was impossible to miss.

My dad wasn't any more convinced than I was, but as far as he was concerned, the premeditated pinching of some random guy at the beach was not worth getting upset over.

"Whatever," I said finally, disgusted with all of them. "I have taken Finn to the beach for the last time."

Finn didn't even look up when he heard this. He appeared to be laboring over a drawing of the two of us at the beach. With my mom's help, he'd written "Caitlin and I swim together" across the top, and he was coloring carefully around all the happy fish he'd added to the ocean. He looked so sweet and harmless I almost gagged. Manipulative little—wait. I looked closer. The happy fish all had fins. And teeth. And they were schooling around *me*!

"Fine, Caitlin," my mom said, using her Very Disappointed voice. "Does this mean *you're* going to clean up the boat while *I* entertain your little brother?"

"Yes!" I exclaimed. "By all that is holy, yes!"

And then I ran in here and hid so she couldn't retract her offer.

Anyway, I'm a much better cleaner than my mom. She and my dad have been outsourcing the household chores for years, and she refuses to let the Merry Maids use any substances that might actually *clean*, on account of not wanting to add to the Chesapeake's oxygen-deprived dead zone. (Because we'd just hate to endanger that painful jellyfish population, now wouldn't we?)

So, as of this moment, I think I'm really starting to get a handle on things. I've worn the yellow bikini. I've successfully launched New Caitlin—and I know I was successful because I immediately attracted the attention of a stunningly hot guy who then invited me to a party. His friends offered to drive me to school, so I've got that all sorted. And I have been relieved of all responsibility for my pestilent little brother. Things honestly could not be bett—wait.

Oh. My. God.

I AM GOING OUT WITH A HOT GUY!!!!

And this isn't just any hot guy, this is TRISTAN. He is quite possibly my *soulmate*. This party will be our first *date*. We will discuss lunar phenomena and deepen our burgeoning (word list shout out!) love. The stakes could not be higher.

Breathe. Breathe. Breeeeathe.

I've never been out with a hot guy before. I mean, I went to Sadie Hawkins last year with Hunter Werro, but that doesn't count because Hunter is *not* hot and he was sort of obligated to say yes because I was tutoring him in Spanish. And Sadie Hawkins isn't a party, it's a school function. With nuns. You definitely can't count it if there are nuns involved.

What am I going to *do*?! I need Shelby.

The Pickled Pirate
The hillside behind the kitchen
9:26 p.m., August 16

FIRST CALL

DURATION: 4 SECONDS

COST: $0.25

It's not easy living at a popular local pub. The only place I could find to conduct a private phone call was behind the main building, where the ground is very steep and the light is very faint. This made it nearly impossible to monitor the area around my flip-flops for approaching hermit crabs, but I'm a trooper. I curled my toes so they posed less of a crustation temptation and held my stopwatch at the ready.

I was hoping to keep this short. Obviously, I could spend hours describing Tristan, but thanks to T-Mobile's repressive international rate structure, it seemed prudent to forgo enumerating his myriad glorious attributes until I was able to send her an email.

Systems check. I squeezed the button on the side of my dad's stopwatch. The digital display lit, bathing the hillside in soft, green light.

Wait, are hermit crabs attracted to light? Fish and bugs are attracted to light, but what about hermit crabs? I hid the stopwatch against my body. Still light! Why was there light by my—oh. I smashed my cell against my cheek so the screen was less visible.

Beep. My face ended the call.

Crab.

Why have I never realized how big my chin is?!

SECOND CALL

DURATION: 3 MINUTES 51 SECONDS

COST: $1

S helby answered on the second ring.

Between my general level of excitement and my concern for my toes (Why am I always wearing open-toed shoes when I encounter fierce wildlife?) it's possible my language skills were not at their sharpest.

"Please pause," she interrupted. "Why are you rambling on about full moons and Ikea? Did they make you join the Sci-fi/Fantasy Club already? I thought your school didn't start until Sep—"

"Nuh-no!" I cut her off, gripping the stopwatch. "The Ikea eyes belong to a *guy*. He's taking me to a full moon *party*. Tomorrow! Whadda I do?"

"Ohemgee, seriously! Amazing! You must have worn the yellow bikini. I *told* you it would look fabulous. You wore it, didn't you?"

The girl attributes mystical powers to the yellow bikini. Hey, maybe she's right. *Something* brought Tristan to me, and I doubt it was my conscientious reapplication of SPF 50.

"Yes," I sighed, "I wore the yellow bikini, okay? You were right about the bikini."

There was a brief silence, then Shelby said, "You better not screw this up."

"Shel!"

"Seriously, if you're not still going to parties with hot guys when I come to visit over Christmas, I'm not going to be your friend anymore."

"*Shelby!*" Sadly, she was too far away to strangle. "Focus! I'm roaming, remember?"

"Oh, right. Sorry. Let me think."

"Think fast," I warned.

"The O'Neill sundress," she pronounced, "with your teal flip-flops. Don't try to wear those sandals with the little heels. You'd totally fall on your butt in them. And, whatever you do, don't talk to anyone about music!"

"O'Neill dress. Teal flops. Got it. Gotta go!"

As I moved the phone away from my ear, I heard her shriek, "*Do not screw up!*"

I took a deep breath. She really should not be yelling at me right now. I'm in a vulnerable state. I need careful nurturing. New Caitlin is a fragile baby tadpole, like the ones you get in the mail from Grow-a-Frog. Forget my Froggy Food and I'll be floating belly-up in my Tadventure Tank before I have the chance to sprout froglet legs. Would it kill her to show a little sensitivity?

Maybe New Caitlin can make some more supportive friends.

The Pickled Pirate
Alone, but not lonely
8:12 a.m., August 17

If you think eating breakfast alone at a bar sounds like a depressing way to start the day, that's only because you've never eaten breakfast with my little brother.

When Finn is sitting still, not ranting or plotting or perpetrating heinous acts, he is—even I must admit—the cutest little boy you will ever see. He has big blue eyes with long, pale lashes, and his red hair curls into soft little ringlets all around his face. Baby cupids look devious compared to Finn.

As his sister, I know what evil lurks beneath his sweetly freckled exterior, and I have natural immunity to his dimpled little smile. Others are not as fortunate.

Like a lantern fish or a Venus fly trap or any of nature's wiliest predators, Finn's appearance gives him a huge advantage when it comes to ambushing unwary prey. It took him less than a day to cozy up to The Pickled Pirate's morning staff, and now the kitchen ladies produce a single, perfect, Mickey Mouse–shaped waffle every morning. Just for Finn.

The kitchen staff is safe (for now anyway) because Finn likes their Mickey waffles. And they think his delight in cartoon-shaped food is sooooooo adorable.

Only because they don't see what I see. They don't have to watch Finn slice off Mickey's ears, one by one, and drizzle the stumps with strawberry syrup. They don't have to listen to him joyfully squealing, "Owwwww! No, no, not my ears!" every morning as he dissects his breakfast.

It's so not the kind of thing anyone should have to endure at 8 a.m.

But today I enjoyed my first gore-free breakfast in nearly a week. My mom and Finn have gone off on a field trip to the rainforest, leaving me in peace with a carafe of syrup (maple, *not* strawberry) and a box full of tools and cleaning supplies.

Life doesn't get much better.

Well, I suppose I could have a hot date with a gorgeous, Ikea-eyed genius tonight. I guess that would be better.

Oh, wait—I *do* have a date with a gorgeous, Ikea-eyed genius tonight! And he has no idea I'm a scrawny freak who skipped third grade. He thinks I'm cool and confident and effortlessly fashionable. Of course, someday I'll *have* to tell him I skipped third grade—not anytime soon, of course, but he's got to know before the wedding. As Brad Pitt and Angelina Jolie demonstrated in *Mr. and Mrs. Smith,* if you base a relationship on lies, you just end up trying to kill each other.

But I bet Tristan won't even *care* that I skipped third grade. Because a guy with his intellectual capital would never be threatened by a smart woman. In fact, I wonder if that's why he asked me out. Maybe he noticed my word list and admired my inquiring nature. Or maybe he was impressed by my reading level. I mean, *Rebellious Passion's* not *Ulysses* or whatever, but it does contain many advanced vocabulary words, and it doesn't skimp on the mature content.

God. I can't believe I'm only fifteen and I've already found my perfect person, the man who values me for my mind. It's like a dream. Hmm. I wonder what his last name is. I bet it's something really swish.

Mrs. Caitlin Davies-Windsor

Not too shabby, right? It makes me sound like one of those rich people from first class on the Titanic. Shelby's going to be soooo jealous. Especially if she ends up with Carson the Tech Crew Boy, who's somehow still hanging in there. His last name is Tickle, and she's not as liberated I am, so she'd end up as Shelby Tickle, which, frankly, sounds pretty steerage. But I would totally let her in my lifeboat because a friend is a friend, even if she marries below her station.

Unghhhhh. I can't believe I have another twelve whole hours before I see Tristan again. Fortunately, I have loads of cleaning to do. Cleaning always takes my mind off my troubles. It's better than

Rebellious Passion. It's better than ice cream. It's better than Ever-note! Cleaning is my jam.

I was six years old when my parents bought our house in An-napolis. The previous owner was a really, really old lady who had basically let the house fall down around her. The siding was rotting off the outside, and inside, everything was covered in dust and cat pee. I told my parents I'd run away before I lived in such a place. But after a solid year of remodeling and untold pots of money spent, we moved into our beautiful, like-new house in Murray Hill. And we all love it. I'm sure *Island Time*, like our house in Annapolis, just needs a little work.

At least I *hope* it just needs a little work because we're moving aboard tomorrow.

My parents actually put in a good effort yesterday while I watched Finn at the beach. They found new cushions for the settees at some boat store in town, and they paid the housekeeper from The Pickled Pirate to come and help with all the scrubbing. The new stove is on order from Puerto Rico because they couldn't find one on-island, but that's fine with me. The Pickled Pirate's ultimate nachos rule.

Dad said the hardest part was clearing all the junk out of the boat. Apparently, every last bin and locker was stuffed with empty cigar boxes. I guess we know what happened to the former owners now: they died of lung cancer. I hear it's a miserable way to go.

But Bertrand has another theory.

"Only one thing all those boxes can mean," he said, sliding cherry and orange slices onto a waiting toothpick.

"What?" I asked, handing him a new toothpick from the box by my elbow.

He shook his head like he didn't want to say, which I didn't be-lieve for a second. Bertrand *always* wants to say.

"Come on, Bertrand, what else could it mean?" He'd already dismissed the only logical explanation I've come up with—namely that the *Island Time*'s former owners were hoarders. Hoarders are people who feel a compulsion to save all kinds of useless stuff, like old newspapers and dead cats and the toys that come in Happy Meals. I've read all about this in Dear Abby, and while it's a serious condition, counseling and medication can help.

He assembled the next fruit kabob and held out his hand for another toothpick. "Little girls shouldn't have to hear of these things, but . . ." He paused dramatically.

My breath caught. "But what?"

"Smugglers," he pronounced in a low voice.

"Smugglers?"

He gave a brusque nod.

I thought for a minute, but couldn't see it. "Smugglers of what? Empty cigar boxes?"

Bertrand rolled his eyes. "Not the boxes. What's *inside* the boxes. The cigars."

I was still confused. "Why, are cigars illegal here?"

"Not here. But in the States, yes."

I shook my head slowly. "No, I don't think they are."

"*Cuban* cigars," he elaborated, "are not legal in the States."

"Oh." Come to think of it, Trevor Noah had mentioned something about the trade embargo against Cuba being reinstated during the late stupidness. But . . .

"But those cigar boxes all say '*Hecho en Miami*,'" I pointed out. And it doesn't take a third-year Spanish student (and two-time winner of the Outstanding Achievement in Foreign Language Award) to translate that one. "Why would anyone smuggle American cigars?"

He tilted his head and gave me a look.

Sometimes I need things spelled out for me, okay? I have limited experience with the criminal mind. Well, okay, I have five years of experience with Finn, but he hasn't progressed to smuggling. Yet.

"They sail to Cuba and buy cigars." Bertrand placed exaggerated emphasis on each word. "Then they take the Cuban cigars and they put them in a box that says American Cigars. Then they take them to the US."

"Oh."

I still think my theory is better. Really, who'd go to all that trouble for stinky cigars?

At any rate, the *Island Time* is now garbage-free and habitable. Or almost habitable. My dad set off a bug bomb in the cabin after finding some cockroaches, so no one can go inside the boat for twenty-four hours. Our move-in date is now scheduled for tomorrow.

It's also why I've decided to spend the day cleaning all the slime and barnacles off the hull of the boat. Obviously, we can live on a boat with a slimy hull. The growth won't affect our quality of life until we decide to sail somewhere, but we don't have any sails right now, so this may not be the most pressing of our issues. Still, I can't work below in the poison-filled cabin, and I've never seen anything that needed cleaning more than the bottom of the *Island Time*. The ick factor is off the charts. I can't resist.

And maybe I don't exactly know what I'm doing, but Sarah Talbert's older brother has been cleaning boat bottoms every summer since he was twelve, and no offense to Sarah, but I've seen racoons more competent than her brother. How hard could it be?

The Pickled Pirate
Showering over and over
1:58 p.m., August 17

Perhaps I underestimated the difficulties involved in the process of slime and barnacle removal. (Though, for the record, Sarah Talbert's brother is still a disaster. I once saw him peel something off the yacht club parking lot and *eat* it. And it wasn't something he'd just dropped, either.)

Outfitted in my snorkeling gear and a black Speedo tank suit, (which, against my pasty skin, makes me look like I drowned three days ago, but whatever. Like the fish were going to care.) I tackled the job with a green scrubby-sponge. I have yet to meet the mess that can't be vanquished with the help of a green scrubby-sponge.

The job started out well enough, but yuuuuuck. As I scrubbed the first section of hull, the water around me filled with grunge, growing murkier and murkier as I worked. Slimy bits of weedy, green algae swirled on the current, catching in my hair, in my ears, even in the edges of my swimsuit. If not for my snorkel, I'd have been choking on the stuff.

After a few minutes, I quit worrying about the grunge cloud because the inside of my mask had fogged over entirely. I could barely make out the hull in front of me, so the water quality hardly mattered. I considered rinsing my mask out, but decided a foggy mask was preferable to a grungy mask and carried on. I had scrubbed my way down almost one whole side of the boat (at least the parts I could reach without scuba gear) when I heard a strange knocking sound. Puzzled, I lifted my head out of the water and slid my mask up onto my forehead.

Several yards away, a dinghy nudged up alongside *Island Time*. A boy stood in the stern, holding on to *Island Time*'s toe rail.

"Hi, Caitlin," he hailed. "Remember me? From the beach?"

"Ayuhh," I said, snatching at the mouthpiece of my snorkel. Oh god, it was covered in little strings of slobber. I swiped my hand across my mouth and rinsed it in the water. Nobody saw that, right? "Yes! Totally. You're Joe. Hi!"

"Jonas," he said, making a face.

"Huh?" I put my hand to my mouth and performed a surreptitious slobber check.

"My name's Jonas," he explained. "No one really calls me Joe."

"Yeah, okay." I nodded. "You just like to be introduced that way. Makes perfect sense."

Oops. That right there was old Caitlin stuff. New Caitlin isn't sarcastic to boys. They perceive it as hostile. Shelby insisted we watch *10 Things I Hate About You* twice in a row to illustrate this point. (Or so she claimed. She doesn't just like that movie, she *loves* it. Like a Prada backpack.)

But Joe—I mean *Jonas*—just smiled.

I guess with a name like Jonas, he'd have to have a sense of humor. Not that it's a *horrible* name or anything. And I can totally see how bad names happen to good people. I'm sure if my dad hadn't gotten a vote, my mom would have named me, like, Ruth Bader Goodall Curie of Aquitaine or something.

But, still, Jonas was a quirky choice. Maybe his parents were really into boy bands, or maybe it was a Bible thing. Wasn't Jonas the name of the guy who got swallowed by the whale? I had to take Old Testament freshman year, but I couldn't remember much in the way of details. Brother Luke let us all pick a section to present on, and I spent most of the semester figuring out how to craft a scale model of the Holy Temple out of sheet cake. My Holiest of Holies was filled with strawberry pastry cream and it was *delicious*.

"I saw someone in the water over here and thought it might be you," he said.

L'il bit stalkerish, but ohhhh-kayyy.

I must have looked a little freaked out, because he pointed to shore and explained, "I live on the hill over there." He then gestured to something in the bottom of his dinghy. "I'm testing out the latest version of my device."

"Oh," I said, relieved. "That's cool."

"You scrubbing barnacles?" He nodded at my scrubby-sponge.

"Ye-es," I answered. Why else would I be swimming around in the middle of a grunge plume?

"Have you done this before?" he asked.

"Nope. First time. But it's really not that hard. I think I've got the hang of it," I said dismissively, ready to get back to it.

"Looks like," he agreed. "But you won't get the barnacles off with that sponge."

Oh, so he came over to tell me my business. Some guys think they know everything. "Oh, really?" I pointed to my grunge plume. "What's all this, then?"

"Algae. Lots of it. But the barnacles are still on there."

Ha. Whatever. I waved my hand to clear the water and examined the section of hull by my shoulder.

"Dang it," I said.

He hid a smile and held out a tool with a wide, flat metal blade. "Here. You need a scraper to get barnacles off."

"Hmm." I applied the scraper to the hull in a long, even stroke. A shower of gray-brown barnacle chips immediately joined my green grunge plume. It was so satisfying, I did it again.

"Yeah. Like that," he encouraged.

"Wow, thank you!" I said, scraping some more. This was amazing. Even better than pressure-washing the driveway. I looked over at Jonas. "Can I borrow this?"

"Sure," he agreed. "I'm going in a bit shallower to run some tests, but I'll stop by for it later."

"What kind of tests?" I asked before I thought better of it. I needed to stay focused. I still had acres of hull to scrape.

He shot me a pleased grin. "I'm working on a device that repels sea turtles, so they don't get caught in fishing nets and drown."

"Oh." I blinked. "Does that happen a lot?"

"Well, fishermen here use TEDs—Turtle Exclusion Devices—which help the turtles escape. But, lot of times, they panic and drown anyway. And some of the turtles are too big to fit through the TEDs. Leatherbacks can be huge, and they're endangered. This device would keep the turtles from swimming near the nets in the first place."

"Wow, that's . . . extremely cool. I'd love to hear all about it. Some other time," I added in a rush, holding up the scraper.

"Sounds good." He paused for a second. "Hey, Tristan mentioned you're coming to the Full Moon Party tonight?"

There was an odd note in his voice. Treading water faster to give myself a boost, I studied his face, absently noting he was pretty cute. Not that I *noticed*-noticed, because my heart is spoken for. But Shelby was one hundred percent right in her predictions of hot island boys. "Yeah."

"Lucas and Enzo can give you a ride over. I said I'd tell you if I saw you."

"Oh." I had kind of expected Tristan to take me, but thinking back, he'd only said he'd see me there. He hadn't mentioned picking me up. Maybe because the party was close by? "Where's the party, again?"

"Cappoon's Bay," he said, naming a beach on the north side of the island. As in: not within walking distance.

"Well, yeah, a ride would be great, then. Tell them thanks."

"You can tell them yourself," he said. "They'll be by about 9:30. I'll show you where to wait."

"Okay, well," I huffed a little. Because even with dive fins, treading water gets hard after you've been doing it for an hour or so. "Great."

Jonas let go of *Island Time*'s rail and shoved off, waiting until he'd drifted well clear of me before starting his engine. "Catch you later, then," he called. "Oh, and, by the way," he raised his voice so I could hear him over the noise of the outboard, "watch out for the shrimp!"

And with that, he zoomed away, leaving me to wonder: watch out for the shrimp? I've read the *Guide to Aquatic Life in the Eastern Caribbean* cover to cover, and I didn't see anything in there about man-eating shrimp. Or venomous shrimp. Or even abnormally large shrimp, because I guess even a shrimp could be scary if it was big enough. Maybe.

I have my doubts about that Jonas guy.

I worked my way back down the side of the boat—the side I'd uselessly scoured with the scrubby-sponge—this time creating an enormous cloud of milky, gray murk. I thought I preferred this to the slimy green murk, but it was a close contest. At last, I reached the stern and hauled myself up onto the stern platform, exhausted. I pulled off my dive fins and mask and set them up on the deck.

The weathered teak tread of the stern ladder felt painfully rough beneath my toes, swollen and tender after hours in the ocean. I hoped the water wrinkles weren't permanent at this point. I reached for the stern rail and something in my dive fin caught my attention. What the . . .? I grabbed it off the deck and peered inside.

"*Ahhhhh!*" I shrieked, dropping the fin like it was hot. "*SHRIMP!*"

Because my dive fin was teeming with teeny, tiny shrimp. The smallest shrimp I've ever seen. Maybe more like krill.

I frantically plopped myself on the edge of the stern platform and dunked my feet and fins in the water. After some vigorous swishing, the shrimp were persuaded to detach and swim away. Whew.

Then I wondered how they'd gotten into my fins. I mean, my fins fit pretty snugly. Just like my bathing su—

With dawning horror, I grabbed the neck of my Speedo and peered down the front.

And screamed and screamed and screamed.

~~~~~~~~~~~

It's hours later, and my skin is still crawling (figuratively, not literally—anymore) with the memory of all those horrible, disgusting, *loathsome* little shrimp.

So it turns out, these shrimp, or krill, or ick, *whatever* they are live in the grassy grunge I spent all morning scrubbing off the hull of our boat. And when I scraped off their home, the legions went looking for another. And I guess my bathing suit, and ears, and hair—oh my god, they must love hair. *All* hair. Gak. I can't think about this anymore! I need another shower.

CHAPTER 8

The Pickled Pirate
Room 4
8:40 p.m., August 17

I don't have a curfew, per se—not because my parents are cool, "anything goes" kind of people. More like it's just never come up. As I mentioned before, I'm not much of a party girl, and the few parties I've been to with Shelby fell on nights when I was sleeping over at her house.

But just because the issue had not previously arisen didn't mean I was expecting my parents to cheerfully wave me off to a party that doesn't even start until ten o'clock. I anticipated plenty of resistance—from my dad—and formulated an airtight argument with him in mind. I also chose my timing based on this expectation, knowing there would come an hour when I would either have to start getting ready or miss the party entirely.

I was counting on it going down something like this:

(Begin 8:10 p.m.)
Me: Announce plans.
Matt: Refuse.
Chorus:

Me: Calm, concise argument.

Matt: Rebuttal.

(Repeat as necessary until 8:20 p.m.)

Me: Matt, I have to start getting ready *right now.*

Matt: Fine, but we're going to have a conversation about this in the morning, young lady.

But, when argument-thirty arrived, my dad was still at the bar watching CNN, and it was my *mom* who had the expected cow. Which is pretty weird considering she's the one who's always talking about how much safer it is here than back in the States, and if Congress would just pass effective gun control legislation, we all could be this safe.

I struggled to regroup, but my Matt-tailored arguments weren't getting me very far with my mom. I finally abandoned them and just improvised.

"Kids here have European sensibilities, Erica. And Europeans do everything later than we do. In Spain, they don't even eat dinner until eleven o'clock at night."

"Okay . . ." she said, looking concerned, "but if you're not leaving here until nine thirty, I can't even imagine what time this party will end. Why does this have to happen so late?"

"It's a Full Moon Party," I explained. "We have to wait for moonrise."

"Oh!" Her expression cleared. "Well, that sounds *fascinating.* I just knew living down here would bring us all closer to nature. And, you know, modern Druids observe certain lunar rituals—"

Then I had to listen to a long spiel about the Coligny calendar, and tides, and the symbolism of lunar transformations . . . whatever. How can I be expected to care about something as trivial as tides? I am going out with Tristan!

And it's going to be so awesome. I can't wait to bask in his gorgeous brilliance. I will laugh at his highbrow jokes and stare deep into his Ikea eyes. I will run my fingers through his golden hair beneath a silvery moon. I . . . crap!

Is that clock right? It can't be. Eight-fifty! I CAN'T GET READY IN FORTY MINUTES!

How can I possibly do all of this in forty minutes: wash my hair again, shave my armpits (I just shaved them yesterday, but my armpit stubble grows really fast), blow-dry my hair, tame the tropically induced frizz with exactly four drops of hair serum, find my MAC *Stranger Things* lip gloss (maybe in that Ziploc I took on the plane?), clip my nails, cover up that red spot on my chin that appeared TONIGHT of all nights, apply deodorant (DO NOT forget deodorant!), apply mascara (after I wipe the excess from the wand with a tissue, like Shelby showed me), find a bra that doesn't show beneath the O'Neill sundress, perform last-minute check for lingering shrimp . . .

Oh god. It's 8:54. GOTTA GO!

The Pickled Pirate
In a rough place
10:47 a.m., August 18

I woke up this morning with a monster case of the flu. I am soooo sick, probably dying of some tropical disease, and my parents are nowhere to be found. They didn't even buy me chicken soup or Gatorade from Thelma's before they went off . . . wherever they went.

But, flu aside, last night was a perfectly executed *dream* . . . up to the point when I started to feel sick. After that, it majorly sucked.

And, okay, it didn't start out all that flawlessly, either.

"No, you're not," my dad said as I tried to leave.

I treated him to my nastiest glare. It's a modified version of Finn's Promise of Retribution look, and I worked hard getting it just right. It's devastating. Not that my dad noticed. He was eyeing the TV above the bar with an irritated expression. "Hey, Bertrand, have you found the remote yet?"

I snapped my fingers to reclaim my time. "As you would see, Matt, if you would only peel your eyes from the unhinged, bombastic rantings of"—I squinted at the screen–"Tucker Carlson. Ew." I looked away, but the image of sentient silly putty lingered. "I am already dressed to go out, because Erica said I could."

"And—" he broke off as Tucker said something particularly duplicitous. One of the guys at the bar threw an onion ring at the TV and the ring slid down the screen, leavening a big smear over Tucker's face. Bertrand made no move to wipe it off.

"*And*," my dad repeated, "I'm sure your mother would back you up on that, but she's asleep. And she is asleep because it is nine-thirty at night, which is a nice hour to go to bed. Not a nice hour to go out."

"I think it's a *glorious* hour to go out. Because it's the hour my ride is arriving to take me to a select gathering where I will engage in stimulating conversation with people who are not intimidated by my intelligence and poise."

At that, my dad finally looked away from the TV. So did the two other guys watching at the bar. (But not, I think, because they were moved by my argument. I suspect they were just tired of laboring to parse Tucker's tortuous logic.)

"Caitlin, you're fifteen. Your blood composition is ninety-five percent hormones. You don't need any more stimulation in your life."

"Umm, excuse me, but haven't you been around for my whole life? Because I would think you'd have noticed somewhere along the way that my life, to this point, has been completely stimulation-free. Stagnant. Fully a dead zone."

"Well, you've survived thus far," my dad said, turning back to the TV. "Why don't you go to bed and we'll find you some stimulation tomorrow?"

"Caitlin?" called a voice from behind me. Footsteps approached. "Oh. Good evening, Dr. Davies."

I turned to see Jonas give my dad a quick wave.

"Wha?" Looking kind of surprised, my dad took in Jonas's outfit of neat, dark jeans and a collared shirt—the equivalent of black tie for the Caribbean in August. "Hi there, Jonas. Are you taking my daughter to this party she's been telling me about?" he asked, sounding considerably more mellow.

"Some friends of mine are giving us a ride," Jonas said.

"Are these friends safe drivers?"

"Yes, very safe."

"And how old did you say you were?"

"I'm making seventeen in November."

"Well, that's okay, then. You two have fun."

And just like that, I was free.

"You know my dad?" I asked Jonas as we walked out to the road.

"We met a couple days ago. I gave him a hand with the outboard on your dinghy."

"Oh. Well, it must have been some hand, then, because he totally wasn't letting me go until you walked up."

He inclined his head. "I also gave him a tow back to the dock. But he'd only been floating around out there for a few minutes." He stopped by a stretch of low stone wall. "They'll pick us up here."

Following his example, I sat down on the wall and waited for my eyes to adjust to the low light. The moon was out and full, but it was very dark where we sat in the shadow of the hill. Around us the coquis chirped their little hearts out, and the longer we sat, the louder they got. I have nothing against frogs, but coquis are so annoying. They wait until you're almost asleep then start with the *cooo-keee, cooo-keee, cooo-keee,* all night long. Someone needs to explain to this species about indoor voices.

"SO," I said loudly, noting with satisfaction the coqui volume immediately decreased, "Jonas is an interesting name. Are you named after the whale guy in the bible?"

He shook his head. "Jonas means 'dove.' It's the territorial bird of the VI. My dad picked it because his boat was named *Dove.* He was a fishing boat captain."

I gasped. "Oh, I'm *so* sorry. He died?" I hoped it wasn't a whale. I know it's probably pretty hard to get swallowed by a whale, on account of them being filter feeders, but long odds are probably cold comfort when you're stuck in a steamy whale stomach.

He gave me a sideways look and burst out laughing. "No! He manages a marina in Road Town now."

"Ohhh," I said. "Well, *that's* good."

"My mom's the chef on a crewed charter," he added. He reached into his shirt pocket and pulled out a small, napkin-wrapped square. "Here." He peeled the napkin back and handed me a cookie. "She made these."

I took a tiny bite. Buttery, vanilla goodness crumbled in my mouth and melted on my tongue.

"These are delicious!"

Jonas nodded and bit into his own cookie. We sat there for a while, munching away, with no sign of our ride. I hadn't brought my phone, but it felt like we'd been waiting for hours. I licked the last crumb from my finger and asked, "Do you think they forgot us?"

"No. They'll be along. They get distracted sometimes."

"Oh." Well, that should make for an interesting year of carpool. I wondered about the tardy policy at St. Hilda's.

The twins finally pulled up—twenty minutes late—in a Range Rover. A very shiny and new-looking Range Rover. I recalled the amount of money we'd paid to import *pillows* into the BVI and applied that percentage to a Range Rover. Holy shrimp.

I turned to Jonas, who shrugged. "It's their dad's. He does investment banking or something."

Jonas and I piled into the back seat and found Tess already in there, looking tree-hugger chic in a flowy black sundress that complimented her light brown skin, and a shell necklace strung with hemp. A thin braid near the front of her face was wrapped in more hemp.

She cut off my greeting with an urgent, "Better buckle up!" and we were off. And I mean *off*. Gravel scattered, dust flew. Had it been daytime, chickens would surely have perished. The Range Rover accelerated from zero to death wish in half a second, and we shot down the road, past the ferry terminal and into the night, where I discovered purple hair and luxury vehicles are not Enzo and Lucas's only distinguishing features. They're also kind of A Lot.

"Sorry we're late," Enzo called from behind the wheel, "I had to give Lucas a haircut."

I glanced at Lucas who was, in fact, notably less purple-haired than he had been the day before. Which is to say, the hair he had was still purple, but there was considerably less of it. And, though I could only see one side of his head from the back seat, what remained looked a little . . . patchy.

But Lucas seemed more concerned with the amount of spam email he'd been getting since Enzo had entered him in an online contest to win a snowmobile.

"Oh, come on," Enzo said. "It's going to be sick. We'll be the only people on Tola with a snowmobile. Maybe in the whole BVI."

Lucas did not disagree about the potential sickness of a

snowmobile in the sunbaked Caribbean. "But now I'm getting, like, three hundred emails a day," he complained.

"Why don't you change your email?" I suggested. Jonas nudged me and shook his head, rolling his eyes.

Lucas swiveled around to face me. "Can't. I have to stay in touch with my business partner in Nigeria."

I blinked. "Oh. Okay."

He continued happily, "All I have to do is give him my bank account number, and he's going to wire ten million dollars into it."

Was he kidding?

Enzo made a screeching left turn onto the mountain road and explained. "Our dad told us we had to get jobs this summer. We're learning to contribute."

"I got the best job ever," Lucas laughed.

"Oh, yeah," his brother said sarcastically. "This'll be even better than your idea to open a rare car museum. Tell her what happened when you bought that Subaru Brat off eBay." Without pausing, Enzo told me himself. "He flew to Miami to pick it up, and the seller had mysteriously moved houses and forgotten to leave any car keys. When he got shirty, they set the dogs on him." He ducked an open-handed swipe. "Ohhh! Not laughing anymore, I see."

"I have an entrepreneurial spirit," Lucas said defensively. "You know, I looked into having that guy killed, but it would have cost more than the car."

They were definitely kidding. I think.

"As if *you* should talk," Lucas rallied. He turned again to address me. "Captain Reading Comprehension applied for his dream job on craigslist . . ."

Enzo stared ahead at the road.

Lucas continued, shaking his head sadly, "Then he changed his mind at the last minute and left a nice family completely hanging."

He turned to his brother and mused, "Do you think they were able to hire another maid on such short notice?"

"Their ad," Enzo fumed, "said: room and board provided, lighthouse keeping. *Lighthouse keeping!* I was tricked!"

"The space is crucial, brother."

And the bickering continued until Jonas suggested they play some music.

"Caitlin, what kind of music do you like?" Tess asked.

Shelby has flat-out *forbidden* me to answer this question. "Oh . . . um . . . you know," I deflected desperately, "a little bit of everything. What do you guys usually listen to?"

Something unfamiliar but loud began blaring from the premium sound system, and the twins fell into a debate about whether caramel and dulce de leche were the same thing. Before too long, we arrived on the outskirts of Cappoon's Bay, where we found the road already lined with cars.

"They are not the same thing. They're made of entirely different ingredients! Tess," Enzo demanded. "Tell him."

Tess threw up her hands. "I don't even know what dulce de leche *is!*"

"WHAT?" Enzo hit the brakes, and we all lurched forward against our seat belts. He turned and glared at Tess. "You're banned!"

Jonas groaned softly. "Not again."

"BANNED I say." Enzo pointed at Tess. "Get out!"

Tess rolled her eyes and exited the car. Lucas thrust open his door and got out as well. "You've got to stop doing that," he told his brother hotly, then slammed the door.

Enzo turned up the music and continued down the road. He found space to park atop a small shrub (may it rest in peace), and we piled out of the car.

"Um, what is this?" I asked as we approached a ramshackle heap.

"This is the Bomba Shack," Jonas answered.

I don't know what a Bomba is, but they sure got the "shack" part right. What a dump. Situated right at the edge of the beach, it appeared to be made entirely of trash.

Because, according to Jonas, it was. "The whole thing is built out of stuff that washed up on the beach," he explained. "You know, tires, driftwood, crushed beer cans. That sort of thing."

An entire corner of the structure seemed to be supported by an FJ mast and an old microwave. "So I see."

I didn't have to ask if this was the party venue. Bright lights? Check. Loud music? Check. Teeming crowds spilling out the doors and into the road? Check.

And while the old Caitlin would never have set foot inside such a rickety, well, *shack*, New Caitlin had to admit that, in the light of the full moon, its graffitied walls vibrating with each thump of the bass, the Bomba Shack looked . . . fun.

"What's it like inside?" I asked. A welcome answer to this question would have been "nontoxic," "structurally sound," or even "easy to evacuate in the event of collapse or conflagration."

"Even better," Enzo promised, pushing me through a doorway. Well, it was really more of an opening than a doorway. The word "doorway" implies there's a door attached.

The inside of the Bomba Shack was as spectacularly junkyard-inspired as the outside. Even the random assortment of chairs and tables looked as if they could have washed up in the last storm. A hand-lettered sign taped to a cash register caught my attention. The sign read:

WE ACCEPT
CASH
CREDIT
DEBIT

GOLD
URANIUM
GOATS
SHROOMS
GOATS ON SHROOMS
NO BITCOIN

Realization hit. "Oh my god," I exclaimed. "This is a bar!"

Jonas gave me a curious look. "Everything okay?" he asked.

Sure. Except I was fifteen years old and partying in a bar. Pretty sure this was how it all went wrong for Miley.

Not that I'd never been in a bar before. I go to bars all the time—like when we're eating in a restaurant, and I have to walk through the bar area to get to the bathroom. And I visit the bar at The Pickled Pirate for breakfast, lunch, and dinner—I practically live there now. But this was, like, a *bar*-bar. And it was full of *high school kids*! Everywhere I looked, kids barely older than me stood around laughing or sat at tables, like they had every right to be in a bar. Most of them were drinking, too—and I don't mean Shirley Temples.

"Caitlin?" Jonas said again.

"I'm fine," I said.

I wasn't. At that moment I wanted nothing more than to be the old Caitlin. To be back in my room at The Pickled Pirate listening to Finn talk in his sleep, incinerating mosquitoes with my Zap It! Racquet, and finishing chapter 19 of *Rebellious Passion*. To get out of this BAR before the cops came.

But at the same time, I hadn't even seen Tristan yet, and he was probably pacing the beach wondering when I—his One True Love—would arrive. *And*, I reminded myself, he was expecting New Caitlin—who's just as intelligent as the old Caitlin—but who's also confident and chill.

Confident and chill.

"I'm fine," I said again, confident and chill.

"Okay," Jonas agreed, but he didn't move away. "You want something to drink?"

I scanned the faces around me, but none of them belonged to Tristan. Enzo had already merged with the crowd.

I shrugged. "Sure. Whatever you're having, I guess."

I followed Jonas to the bar, where he spoke to one of the bartenders. A moment later he handed me a squat brown bottle.

I gawked at him. "Is this *beer*?"

Jonas leaned closer so he could hear me over the throbbing music. I repeated my question. Loudly.

"Ginger beer," he shouted near my ear. "You said you wanted what I was having." He held up an identical bottle.

I gazed at the bottle in his hand. "Aren't you worried we'll get caught?" I gestured to the crowd behind us. "Isn't *anyone* worried?"

Jonas looked puzzled for a second, then laughed. "That's right. The drinking age in the States is twenty-five or something, right?"

"Twenty-one," I corrected.

"Here it's eighteen, and they barely enforce it." He clinked his bottle against mine. "Congratulations, you're free to make bad choices."

"Yay!" I said faintly.

He leaned even closer and said, "You're also drinking ginger beer." His lips quirked. "It's nonalcoholic."

Ohthankgod. I cannot be a drunk at fifteen. My parents would never spring for a swishy Malibu rehab facility. I'd end up in some dismal youth-dungeon run by Catholic Charities.

The music grew even louder. "Come on," Jonas half-yelled. "I see Tess there."

Clutching my ginger beer, I trailed behind him through the crowd, avoiding bodies and elbows when necessary. The problem with being five foot one is that, at fifteen, most of my peers have out-grown me. This means they usually aren't watching out for someone eight inches below their line of vision. Unless they were raised in a barn, they apologize *after* they run me over, but I find it's best for everyone involved if I keep a sharp eye out and take evasive maneu-vers when necessary.

Jonas led me without incident to the far side of the bar, where tables by a cutout wall overlooked the beach. Enzo sat at one of these tables, staring resignedly across it at Tess.

"What do you call a fish with no eyes?" she asked as we walked up.

"What?" Enzo moaned.

"Fsssh!" She laughed hysterically.

Enzo spotted us and hopped up.

"There you are!" He marched over and slung an arm around my shoulder. Before I could object, he grabbed my ginger beer and chugged it down. "Oops," he belched discreetly, "looks like you're empty. I'll get you another."

Tess grinned as she watched him walk away, then patted the back of the chair beside her. "Sit, sit!"

I plopped down gingerly on the wobbly wooden chair, and Jonas took the adjacent one.

"What do you get when you cross an elephant with a rhino?" Tess asked.

"Uhh . . ." I glanced at Jonas, who gave me a small smile, "what?"

"El-if-I-no!" Tess burst into laughter. Really loud laughter. Louder than the music, even.

Fearing for my ear drums, I angled away, laughing helplessly. Not at the joke—that was terrible—but at Tess. The way she laughed, so joyful and raucous, at such a stupid joke? Well, it was kind of great.

"She laughed, she laughed!" Tess exclaimed, throwing an arm around my shoulders. "I knew we were going to be friends."

"What are you drinking?" I asked her. I thought I should know so I could steer clear.

"Just Coke. I don't drink alcohol." She chuckled, "Don't need to."

I nodded agreement. Tess was a party all by herself. "Hey, I should look around," I said, "I'm supposed to be meeting someone."

"She's looking for Tristan," Enzo announced, setting a fresh ginger beer in front of me and sliding back into his seat. He turned to me. "Tess is Tristan's stepsister."

Wow, small world. Island. Whatever.

"Are you sure you want to do that?" Tess asked me.

"Do what?"

"Find Tristan."

I laughed. This girl was a riot. "Yeah," I answered, careful to keep my tone casual, like I hadn't been counting the hours until I saw him again. Confident and chill. "Pretty sure."

She shrugged and pointed at a corner of the room. "He's over there," she said, but she was staring at Jonas. In fact, I realized, they were sharing a *look*. I suddenly felt like an idiot for sitting between them on the ride over. And here I was, doing it again!

I hopped up, promised to catch them later, and made my way to the back of the Bomba Shack, where I found Tristan sharing a table with Byron, the sleepy guy from the beach . . . and Onessa and Viv, the girls from the school parking lot.

Where's a crucifix when I really need one?

Viv raised a perfect eyebrow. "Yes?"

"Uhh . . ." Okay, I admit: in that moment, I was not feeling confident and chill. I was feeling distinctly old Caitlin-ish.

Tristan turned my way. "Hey, there you are!"

I looked down into his shining Ikea eyes and golden face and knew this was True Love, the real deal like Jack and Rose, or Bert and Ernie.

"I've been looking everywhere for you! I was starting to worry," he said. "I was just describing you to Onessa and Viv, here, asking if they'd seen you."

Onessa and Viv stared at me through narrowed eyes. And still looked gorgeous.

"Oh," I said, surprised, "Well, I was just over—"

"No worries." He stood and grabbed my hand. "Let's get you a drink. What'll you have? Another?" he asked, nodding at the bottle in my hand. "Or something else?"

"Um," I said, "something else." I really liked the intense flavor of my ginger beer—it was sharp and bright and had really opened up my sinuses—but it made me feel distinctly belchy.

"Like?" he prompted.

"Uh . . ." My gaze landed on the cup in Viv's hand. "What are you having?" I asked her.

"Malibu Coke," she said in a bored tone.

Oh, I loved flavored Cokes. I always ordered a vanilla-flavored one when Shelby and I went to Johnny Rockets. "I'll have one of those," I said.

"Brilliant." He gave me a huge smile. "Let's go."

Interlacing his fingers with mine, Tristan pulled me back to the bar, which was even more mobbed than it had been earlier. I guess gorgeous geniuses have a knack for this sort of thing, though, because a path to the bar opened before him like magic.

He flagged down a bartender and a minute later passed me a plastic cup of Coke, keeping a beer—a real beer—for himself.

"Thanks." I felt a gingery burp coming on but managed to hide it behind a big sip of soda.

"Wow, this is really good!" I said, surprised. I'd never had coconut-flavored Coke before.

He gave me a tender smile, and my heart did a little flip in my chest. My hands started to sweat, and a bubbly feeling churned beneath my ribs.

"Come on," he said, "it's loud in here. Let's go out and have a look at that moon."

Still holding my hand, he led me outside and down the beach, away from the crowd. We found a spot right above the high-water mark and sat in the sand.

Beneath the full moon, enormous and white in the tropical sky, the ocean was a pale, glassy pond. Tiny waves lapped gently against the sand, every third or fourth set coming just high enough to tickle my feet and ankles. It was the most beautiful night of my life. Almost as beautiful as Tristan.

His thumb rubbed against my palm as he casually sipped his beer. "So, what kind of music d'you like?" he asked.

Oh god, *why*? Why does everyone have to ask me that question?! The bubbly feeling below my ribs shut off like a broken fish tank filter. I took a hearty sip of coconut Coke so I'd have a reason for not answering immediately. Then I took another.

You see, Shelby's absolutely right to forbid me from discussing this; the music question is not one I can answer correctly. Not that there's a single right answer, necessarily, but there are definitely wrong answers. And I have all the wrong answers. Musically speaking, I have the taste of your average second grader. And most guys don't find the soundtrack to *Muppet Treasure Island* nearly as cool as I do. Unfortunately, Shelby did not advise me on *how* to avoid this question.

All at once, it came to me. Inspired, I drained my plastic cup and held it to the moonlight.

Tristan blinked. "Ahh . . . looks like you're empty."

"Yep. Too much sodium at dinner." I hung my head as if ashamed of my poor dietary choices. "I'm gonna run and get another one."

"No, no." Tristan nabbed the cup from my hand. "My treat. You wait right here, and I'll be back in a sec."

It didn't seem fair to let Tristan buy my drinks all night. Sodas down here cost a fortune. I thought I at least ought to pay for every other round. But, somehow, I couldn't quite work up the energy to go after him. The gently breaking waves were soft, crystal shushes along the hard-packed sand. And the moon was so *shiny*. A million times shinier than it ever was back in Annapolis. And the stars! I hadn't known there were that many stars in all of space. I braced my arms and leaned back so I could take in the starry, spacey vastness.

Pish, pish, pish, pish. Footsteps sounded across the sand. Once again, like the first time we met, I found myself staring up into blazing Ikea eyes. Though less blue in the silvery moonlight, they somehow seemed more intense than ever.

"Here you are, gorgeous." He held out my Coke, then sat back down beside me. "Enjoying yourself?"

"Absolutely," I said.

"Good." He leaned very close. "I like to see you enjoying yourself."

My mouth suddenly felt very dry. Desert dry. Drier than the Safe Harbor Marina pool after Labor Day. My tongue felt stuck to the back of my teeth. I took another huge gulp of Coke.

"Maybe you should set that down for a sec." Tristan reached out, took the Coke from me, and screwed it into the sand so it stayed upright. Then, his gaze locked with my own, he slowly leaned in and set his lips against mine.

Okay, I probably don't need to tell you that this was my first kiss. If you've been reading carefully—or at all—you'll have already guessed this. Not that I'm a hideous troll or anything. I've even had the occasional compliment thrown my way. Baker Monaghan once told me I was cute like a hamster. And Baker *really* loves his hamsters.

But despite my rodential allure, this happened to be my first kiss.

Fortunately, it wasn't my last. Tristan saw to that immediately. And, holy shrimp, it was AMAYYYYYZINNNNG. His lips were so firm and warm, and after a couple of minutes, I had more than lips to deal with. A tongue was introduced to the equation!

I tried to be cool about it, but I was actually kind of shocked by that tongue. Not that it felt bad or anything. I just needed a moment to get used to the newness of it all. But then I started to feel dizzy. And it wasn't the good, "he kissed her until she was dizzy" sort of dizzy that you read about in pirate romance novels. At least, I don't think it was. It was more like, "I feel weird and possibly nauseous" kind of dizzy. Like when I got out of bed for the first time after having a stomach bug for three days.

So I told him, "I feel dizzy."

"Oh." Tristan lifted his head and looked me over. "Maybe it's your drink."

I knocked back a mouthful of Coke to check. "No, it tastes great. But I'm definitely feeling worse."

He took a quick step back. "Why don't I go get you a water?"

That sounded like a nice idea. Even with the horrible whizzing in my head, I could still appreciate his voice, and his devastating accent. And my mouth was so dry, even worse than before. I was starting to feel extremely bad.

"Actually," I said, "I think need to leave now. Could you take me home?"

"Oh," he said slowly, his voice leaden with disappointment. My heart wept. "But if I take you home now, I won't have time to come all the way back here. It's too far. And I'm giving my sister a ride home, so she'd have to leave early as well."

"Your sister?" I didn't want to make a bad impression on my future sister-in-law.

"Tess."

Tess was good people. Tess would probably forgive me but, god, New Caitlin couldn't be a party pooper! That's not cool. That's not chill. But I just—oh—I felt *awful*. My brain was swishing around inside my head, the world was swishing around outside of it, and closing my eyes just made it swish harder.

"I'm really sorry, but—"

"Tell you what," Tristan interrupted, tenderly smoothing my hair back from my forehead. "You wait here while I run and get you that water. Then we'll see how you feel."

That seemed reasonable. I didn't want to ruin his night, or Tess's. And walking to his car seemed like a tough proposition at that moment. To be honest, sitting upright seemed like a tough proposition at that moment.

"Okay," I said, flopping back in the sand.

Tristan walked off toward the bar, and I stared up at the stars, careful not to let my eyes shut. But then, somehow, they shut themselves, and that felt like an improvement. It was certainly darker that way.

~~~~~~~~

C aitlin? Are you okay?" I opened my eyes and found Tess leaning over me. She was probably furious that she'd have to leave early, and it was all my fault.

"Oh my god." I groaned. "I'm so sorry. I hope I'm not ruining your night."

"Why would you be ruining my night?" She didn't sound angry, just curious.

I groaned softly. "It's just that I really need to go home. I feel really, really bad. And your brother—"

"Stepbrother," she interrupted.

"Huh?"

"He's my stepbrother."

Oh, for the love of—my death might be imminent, and this girl was nitpicking? "Fine. I know your *stepbrother's* your ride, too, and—"

"He's not my ride," she interrupted. "Doesn't look like he's your ride, either."

"What?"

"Mostly everyone's gone. Cleared out and went back to Viv's house to swim in her pool. I'm pretty sure I saw him leave with Byron."

I tried to sit up.

"She has a lovely pool," she explained. "The horizon kind, with the infinity edge."

I glanced down the beach. Sure enough, the Bomba Shack was considerably quieter than it had been just a few minutes earlier.

"But I . . . he said—" Ugh. I felt too ill to argue with her anymore. I shut my mouth and did another sand flop.

I heard Tess sigh and walk away.

Fine, I'd just lie here. What was the point in moving? Tristan had obviously decided I was a drag, and I didn't feel up to a car ride, anyway. I could just sleep here in a miserable heap under the full moon, then catch a taxi home in the morning.

Although I'd never slept on the beach before. Were there nighttime beach predators? In Maryland we had sand fleas, but I didn't think sand fleas would bother me right then. Because, honestly, my arms and legs felt kind of numb. There might have been fiddler crabs crawling all over me, for all I could tell.

Fiddler crabs. I sat up with a jerk. Ooh. Bad idea. Very bad idea. I eased back down and felt the world lurch back into its previous orientation. Fine. Maybe the fiddler crabs would carry me off in the night, and maybe they wouldn't. I didn't have it in me to care.

Oh, but what about my teeth? How was I going to brush my

teeth? I never went to bed without brushing my teeth! It made me have that dream where all my teeth fell out. And it's not like they fell out all at once. First, they'd get loose, and I'd try to hold them in place, but then they'd start to crumble, and I'd end up telling myself that it was okay, that, these days, false teeth screwed right into your jaw and looked perfectly natur—

Pish, pish, pish, pish. Footsteps crossed the sand again.

"Just leave me here, Tess," I moaned. "Let the crabs take me."

"That would be too bad," a deep voice said. "You just got here."

I cracked one eye and saw Jonas hovering over me.

He surveyed me for a long moment. "Got into it, eh?"

"What?" I croaked.

"Got drunk," he clarified.

"Me?" I gasped, shocked to my very core. He might as well have asked me if I smoked crack. (Incidentally, I believe the penalties back at Our Lady of Perpetual Sorrows are the same for both infractions.) "No way! I had two ginger beers and some Cokes. That's *it*."

Jonas reached down and pulled my Coke out of the sand. He held it up to his nose and sniffed.

Jonas is certainly no Tristan, but he looked very cute when his nose wrinkled up like that. I decided to tell him. "You look cute when you do that thing with your nose."

"Ugh. Malibu," was all he said.

I let my eyes close. "Maybe *you've* been drinking. Because this is Tortola, you know. California is, god, I don't know, like five thousand miles away."

Jonas rolled his eyes. "Don't go anywhere." And with that, he walked off down the beach. Leaving me there. In the sand.

Story of my life. Story of tonight, anyway. And *still* no water. I reached out for my Coke but found it gone. Jonas must have taken it with him. Dirty thief.

I shut my eyes and waited for death—or the fiddler crabs—to take me.

Multiple feet crossed the sand.

God, would it never end? I was trying to die, here! Can't a girl be consumed by crabs in peace? But I could feel people staring down at me, so I had to open my eyes.

Jonas and the twins stood over me.

"Gosh, your hair sure is patchy," I greeted Lucas. "I can see your scalp."

Jonas's mouth tipped up at one corner.

"Did she say 'gosh'?" asked Lucas.

"Is she delirious?" asked Enzo.

"Drunk, I think," Jonas said.

I was irate. "I already told you, I've never touched alcohol *in my life!*" I don't even drink the communion wine. My dad says that's a great way to get herpes.

But they weren't listening. I shut my eyes and resolved to never open them again.

"Did she get roofied?"

"I don't think he's that much of a toolbox. Just Malibu, I'm thinking."

"That's worse than drugs, if you ask me. Like drinking suntan oil."

"Hey, remember the time I bet you five dollars you wouldn't drink that bottle of suntan oil, and you did? Is this how you felt?"

"Shut up, clown truck."

"Hey, now, that's not nice. But I'm going to cut you some slack because someone gave you a very bad haircut."

I heard scuffling sounds, and a sprinkling of sand showered my arm.

"Hey. Hey! Back to the problem at hand: what are we going to do with her?"

"Let's write on her. I've got a marker."

At that, I really, *really* wanted to open my eyes, but they wouldn't cooperate. Tell me, what kind of monster writes on a sick person with a marker? That's what drinking alcohol will do to you—turns you into a marker-wielding degenerate.

"Whisky, beer, boozes," I groaned. For some reason, my garbled words weren't aligning with my clear thoughts. I gave it another shot. "Devil brew, no good for you."

Someone laughed. "Lucky thing she's so little."

And that's all I remember. The End.

I think I might need to throw up now.

CHAPTER 9

Soper's Hole Marina
In the Laundromat
3:30 p.m., August 18

This morning my parents moved all our stuff out to the *Island Time*. I would have helped, but I was still feeling absolutely wretched. Instead, I sat at the bar megadosing vitamin C and lamenting how the most romantic night of my life had gone so horribly wrong at the end. I didn't blame Tristan for leaving me on that beach. I had *kissed* him while experiencing symptoms of illness. I knew exactly how reckless that was—that's how my cousin got mono!

It was this living with chickens, that's what it was. It just wasn't healthy to live in such proximity to barnyard fowl. You'd think doctors would know better, but I guess my mom doesn't see a lot of chicken-borne illness inside the beltway, and my dad only teaches.

I shared these thoughts with my dad when he stopped by for a bottle of water.

"Forget the chickens. Let's talk about you coming home drunk, young lady."

"*Drunk?*" I coughed, spraying my orange juice across the bar. "What are you talking about? I'm sick, not drunk."

"You're not sick, you're hungover. And last night you were drunk."

"Matt." I wiped the OJ up with a paper napkin. "There is no conceivable way I was drunk. I consumed nary a drop of alcohol." Jonas had assured me ginger beer was nonalcoholic. And after that I'd switched to yummy coconut Coke.

"By the looks of you, I find that hard to believe."

"Well, believe it!" I cried, deeply offended. Shifting to my knees, I leaned over the bar and tossed the used napkin in the trash can. As I opened my mouth to demand Matt name his seconds, my gaze caught on one of the bottles behind the bar. I peered at the white bottle with the palm-tree-at-sunset logo and suddenly recalled a hazy snippet of dialogue from the night before.

My mouth snapped shut, and I sat back down on my bar stool. Well. I cleared my throat. "And even if I had, it's legal here, you know."

"It's legal for people over the age of eighteen. Last time I checked, young lady, you were barely fifteen years old."

Okay, well that's true. But it's partially thanks to him that I must face the same pressures as kids sixteen and older. He totally could have stood up for me in second grade when they decided to skip me. But he didn't. He was probably busy experimenting on animals or something.

"Not that it matters," I informed him, "because I have no intention of touching alcohol." *Ever again*, I added silently.

"Damn right you're not. Because that was your last party. You don't need to be hanging around with older kids who drink and do god knows what else."

"Whatever." I laid my aching head on the cool, varnished bar top. Now that Tristan thinks I'm a plague-ridden loser—or, worse, a drunk—why would I want to go to any more parties? And my dad's bedside manner is *terrible*. It's a good thing they don't let him near any patients.

The sugar from the OJ kicked in, and I felt a little better after breakfast, so I volunteered to do laundry. The marina complex across the harbor has a coin-operated laundromat that, on a weekday in the middle of August, was completely deserted. I filled all four washers with our stuff and struck out in search of coffee.

The Soper's Hole Marina is fully the cutest thing I've ever seen. The buildings, with their colorful shutters, gingerbread trim, and elaborate railings, look like a colonial-era West Indies harbor town. (Except without the open sewers and yellow fever.) The complex offers shops, restaurants, watersports rentals, a supermarket, a spa, and offices for the charter companies that base out of the marina. Best of all, they have Wi-Fi.

My coffee quest suffered a temporary delay when I spotted the world's cutest swimsuit cover-up in the window at Arawak. It was eighty-six dollars, which seemed like a lot for a swimsuit cover-up, but I would gladly have paid twice that to never have to show my butt at the beach again. Then I bought a double latte from Omar's and went in search of a really quiet place to sit and coddle my lingering coconut rotgut headache. After poking around a bit, I found an empty table just outside one of the charter offices. Not much traffic was going through that door in August. I moved a chair into the shade and pulled out my phone.

It was time to report in to Shelby about my Full Moon Party disaster. It had to be done. But I hated to disappoint her after all the time she'd invested in this project. And I'd been doing so well until I, uh, became indisposed.

Maybe I could leave that part out.

But Shelby was sure to ask about Tristan, and the devastating reality of the situation was that he might not be so interested after last night.

I mean, the damage was done. There was no need to ruin Shelby's afternoon. We could talk later. I closed FaceTime and opened Safari.

One thing's for sure: if, after last night's carnage, I somehow manage to pull New Caitlin out of the fire, I am going to be *prepared* next time The Big Question comes up. No, not the one about the meaning of life. (The answer is ice cream. Duh.) The one that goes, "So, what kind of music do you like?"

Well, I don't know the answer to that. I somehow doubt the old Caitlin's musical tastes would suit New Caitlin.

Although surely even New Caitlin listens to the *Newsies* soundtrack. Shelby can have her Big Feelings about *Mamma Mia* but, honestly, *Newsies* is by far the superior film. I mean, it ticks all the boxes: two hours of fit teenagers singing, dancing, and fighting the exploitation of underage labor. Hoo, yeah, seize that day! Plus, Christian Bale was, like, seventeen when they filmed *Newsies*, so I can realistically daydream about Jack Kelly taking me to senior prom. (Because we're only allowed to bring prom dates who are still in high school.)

So maybe New Caitlin still has *Newsies* favorited, but I also needed something with broader appeal, something I could mention without raising any eyebrows. Probably something without singing Muppets.

The answer came to me as I walked back to the laundromat through Pusser's, where Bob Marley was blaring through the speakers to an empty restaurant. Oh, that was perfect. What could be cooler than Bob Marley? Everyone loves Bob Marley!

After changing the laundry over, I created a playlist of Bob Marley and the Wailers' greatest hits, bought a water (cost: $3) from the market, and returned to my table by the charter company office.

But the peace of the charter company office had been broken. A loud voice poured from the open doorway. "I'm telling you, I paid for a seven-night charter!"

Oh, I recognized that voice. I peered into the office and, sure enough, the enraged white guy I'd seen at The Pickled Pirate a few days ago stood at the desk, railing at the employee behind it.

"Mr. Fuller." The lady behind the desk looked like she'd had enough for four days. "I understand. All of our charters are seven-day charters."

"Well, then why did you give us a boat only equipped for three?"

She studied him with a bewildered glare. "What?"

"We've been anchoring every night. This Boaty Ball system is garbage!"

"That's fine. You're authorized to anchor in any marked anchorage."

"I'm telling you, we weren't provisioned correctly! It's been three nights, and you only gave us three anchors. What are we supposed to do now?!"

The lady's appalled expression indicated this conversation could last awhile. I grabbed my stuff and moved to a table at the other end of the sidewalk. It was hotter away from the breeze but considerably less shouty. I leaned back in my chair and shut my eyes.

"Isn't that the girl from last night?"

Ugh, now what?

"What, you don't recognize that awful home-color job?"

I cracked an eye and spied Onessa and Viv seating themselves at a table farther down the sidewalk.

Were they talking about me? My hair is *not* colored. Who would purposely dye their hair to look like Maryellen Larkin?

"I was too busy noticing those pit stains." I could feel Onessa's side-eye inside my skull, that's how strong it was. "Do all Americans go around in public looking like that?"

I looked down at my gray Our Lady of Perpetual Sorrows gym shirt. Okay, so there might have been some subtle staining, but it wasn't *that* noticeable.

"Probably."

At this point I was more than ready to slink away with dignity, but I couldn't leave the laundry and I was out of tables.

"But I saw her on the beach with Tristan. That's major."

Onessa snorted in disagreement. "Minor."

And, anyway, I reminded myself, New Caitlin doesn't slink. She doesn't hide in libraries. She's confident. She's chill. She's above the petty aspersions of hostile peers.

"She's temporary," Onessa continued. "Just some boat girl. Live-aboard rubbish."

Excuse me?? Living on a sailboat may be a little unconventional, but it is a perfectly valid lifestyle choice. I am not "live-aboard rubbish." I am *yachtwardly mobile.*

I turned to Onessa and Viv and gave them a big smile. "Oh, *hi.* Viv and Onessa, right? The bar girls!" I was going for maximum friendliness, though I suspect the result was more Bruce the Shark.

For a minute they just sat there looking surprised, then Onessa tilted her head and shot me her own fakey smile. "Hiiiii."

Viv picked up the ball. "So great we keep running into you. Since you'll be at our school this year." She put subtle emphasis on the word "our."

I just raised an eyebrow. Well, I tried to raise an eyebrow, but I can't actually do that, so I raised both eyebrows. "Can't wait."

Onessa tapped in. "You'll be in grade nine, right?"

My smile got bigger. "Eleven, actually." Fish are friends. Fish are friends.

"Oh, a classmate!" she said with phony surprise. "I wouldn't have guessed. You look so *young.* Baby-faced. I bet you get that *all the time.*"

Sadly, I do. Usually followed by something like, "Well, you'll love that when you're older." Like that helps.

"Totally. But at least it's my only face." Oh sweet cheezits. I tried for "confident and chill" and suddenly I was channeling Veronica Lodge. "Soooo, what are you two up to today?"

"Shopping for bathing suits for the Last Bash, of course," Viv sniffed.

"Last Bash?"

"You *have* heard about the Last Bash, haven't you?" They shared a look.

"I might have. I can't recall," I said in a bored tone. I studied my fingernails, then subtly balled my hands into fists. Apparently, barnacle scrubbing is not great for manicures.

Viv laughed again, a tinkling little *ha ha ha*. "Well, you'd *know* if you'd heard about it. Everyone goes to—"

"Oh, would you look at the time!" I interrupted, snatching up my phone as I stood. The Last Bash sounded suspiciously like a party, and I'd had enough partying to last me through college—possibly graduate school. Also, this conversation was super stressful. "This has been so fun. We should meet for coffee sometime."

"Sure," Viv agreed, with zero enthusiasm.

"Yeah, that'd be *sick*," Onessa simpered. "We heard you're a big fan of drinking . . . coffee."

I felt every drop of blood in my body rush to my face. Had they *heard*? *How* had they heard. No, no, noooo! "Okay, well . . . awesome!" I choked out. "We'll get something on the books."

And, with that, I fled to the laundry.

Island Time
On deck
5:25 p.m., August 19

Now that I've been a live-aboard for a full twenty-four hours, I'm distressed to report there are drawbacks to this lifestyle that hadn't previously occurred to me. And I'm not just talking about sharing a cabin with Finn. I was, after all, sharing a room with Finn at The Pickled Pirate, so not much has changed there. (Of course, our cabin is maybe a tenth the size of our room at The Pickled Pirate, but whatever. Seventy-five bucks is seventy-five bucks.) No, I have other complaints, most of them, I regret to say, hygiene related.

For one thing, bathing in the ocean isn't nearly as romantic as it sounds in that pop song that's always playing at my dentist's office. I'm sure Savage Garden *would* like to bathe with me in the sea—once. Then they'd wise up. Because let me tell you something about salt water: it is the enemy of a good lather. My shampoo-plus-conditioner might as well be Vaseline for all it works in the ocean. And when I dropped my Kiehl's Ultra Facial Hydrating Cleansing Bar this evening, it bounced right off the stern platform and sank in twenty feet of water (cost: $18).

Another problem with bathing on the stern platform: it requires standing on the back of the boat, in full view of anyone who happens to pass by in their dinghy. Wearing a bathing suit, obviously, but to wash the bits *under* my bathing suit, I have to stick my hand down there and soap up in full view of the yachting public. And doesn't *that* make a pretty picture for passers-by.

Then, after my not-so-cleansing dip in the ocean, I am allowed to rinse off under the stern-platform's freshwater hand-shower for exactly twenty seconds. My dad stands there and counts. And, okay, so I guess I can understand his stinginess. Our whole water supply is stored in tanks, and when the tanks run out, they have to be filled up with a hose at the nearest fuel dock (cost: $0.15/gallon.) But twenty seconds is *nothing*. If I suck on the ends of my hair, I can still taste the salt. And there's salt residue in my ear, too. And it itches.

But the hygienic shortcomings do not end there, I'm afraid. If you think about it for a minute, you will realize that sailboats are not connected to sewers or anything. They're just out there, floating around. Most boats have holding tanks, which contain the stuff you flush. But the *Island Time* is not so advanced. We have fuel tanks, and freshwater tanks, and that's it. So anything that, you know, comes out of the plumbing . . . pretty soon it's out there floating around, too. And when you're in a harbor like this one, with other boats and people swimming and stuff, it's bad etiquette to flush anything that doesn't, umm, *blend* with the water. So bathroom breaks can require taking the dinghy in to The Pickled Pirate.

Actually, many things require dinghying in to The Pickled Pirate. Eating dinner, for example. Because we still have no stove. We have a refrigerator, so cereal and sandwiches are available on board, but The Pickled Pirate will continue to supply most of our meals until man's red fire comes to the *Island Time*.

Oh, *and* it still smells funny down in the cabin. Even with all the cigar boxes gone. Even after a second cleaning. Which is why I'm sitting on deck at dusk, even though, by doing so, I risk being drained dry by the no-see-ums.

And now my mom's up here, all, "Will you look at that sunset! Isn't this amazing, Caitlin? It's so nice to be settled in finally."

I want to go home.

Soper's Hole Marina
Outside Rite Way
11:40 a.m., August 20

Caitlin, we're out of turkey, and Finn and I are going snorkeling. Can you take the dinghy and get some lunch meat from the market?" my mom asked this morning.

"Sure." No turkey, after all, means no lunch for me. "From where?"

My mom was attempting to spackle Finn with sunscreen while Finn dodged and writhed. "Finn, stop being such a drama llama."

"Drama Llama *bites* and *rips off eyeballs!*" he growled.

"Never mind, I'll find it," I said.

But buying cold cuts in the British Virgin Islands is not the same simple process it is back home.

"Yes?" the lady behind the deli counter asked.

"Could I please have a half pound of sliced turkey?"

"No," she said.

Seriously, just "no." That was it. I stood there gaping for long enough that I guess she felt pressed to explain.

"I got a meeting," she elaborated. And with that, she disappeared through a door into the back.

Who knew deli clerks had such demanding careers?

I was sitting on a planter outside the market, waiting for the meeting to conclude, when Tess appeared and plopped down beside me.

"What do you call a deer with no eyes?" she asked, by way of greeting.

"Dunno. What?"

"No eye-deer!" She barely got the punchline out before the giggles started. "Okay, okay. What do you call a deer with no eyes and no legs?"

"Umm . . ."

"*Still* no eye-deer." This time she threw her whole head back and nearly fell off the planter she was cackling so hard.

She wiped her eyes, gasping a little. "There's a follow-up to that one, but it's really filthy. If you want, though—"

"No," I said quickly, "that's cool. What brings you over here?" She'd explained in the taxi the other day that she and her mom live with Tristan and his dad on the other end of the island, closer to school.

"Yoga again." She gestured to her loose shorts and T-shirt. "What are you up to?"

I told her about the turkey. "And please don't say anything about Island Time, because then I'd have to scream."

She shook her head sympathetically. "Come on, let's get some lunch."

We got sandwiches from Omar's and dug in.

"I ran into Viv and Onessa the other day," I told her, my mouth full of veggie wrap.

She rolled her eyes. "Like I said before, don't worry about them. Onessa's just worried Tristan likes you. Otherwise they'd ignore you."

"They seem a little . . ." Snotty. Poisonous. Like psychotic egomaniacs. "Intense."

Tess shrugged. "Just tell them to go kick a rock. So, are you feeling all recovered? You were pretty trashed the other night."

I nearly choked on my sandwich. "Oh," I coughed, "are we telling this story?"

Tess chuckled. "We are most definitely telling this story."

I dropped my head into my hands. "I had no idea there was rum in my Coke. I thought it was some regional variety. Like that orange flavored Coke they have in Latvia." I peeked at her from between my fingers. "Is anyone else telling this story? Like Jonas, or the twins?" I sat up with a jerk. "Oh my god. I didn't, like, throw up in their car or anything, did I?"

"No, but Enzo said you drooled on Jonas's shoulder."

So now I'm just going to go die. After I get my turkey.

CHAPTER 10

Island Time
Deadly bored with living aboard
4:40 p.m., August 20

When I made my deal with the devil, I may have failed to give due consideration to the specifics of sharing a head with Finn. I'd been so focused on other logistics—clothing storage, reading lights, privacy rules, investing my ill-gotten gains—that I hadn't given the bathroom situation much thought.

Back home in Annapolis, we each have our own bathrooms, but it's not like I've never shared with Finn before. I've shared hotel rooms with him lots of times. But the thing about hotel rooms— even hotel rooms at The Pickled Pirate—is that a housekeeper comes in every day and cleans them.

And the thing about sailboat heads is they're really, *really* small. Like, I can span the whole room with my arms, and my arms are pretty short. The head I share with Finn has a small toilet jammed in next to a tiny sink. Mounted on the wall next to the toilet is a hand shower, and there's a drain in the floor. So, basically, if you wanted to, you could do everything you can do in a bathroom, all at the same time. Not that I have. Because that would be gross.

The reason I bring this up, and I'm aware it's kind of indelicate, is so you can see where I'm coming from when I say this is not the bathroom I would choose to share with a grubby little boy. It's hard to overlook the unrinsed toothpaste spit in our grapefruit-half of a sink. It's hard to overlook the discarded Underoos covering the doormat-sized floor. And it's *really* hard to ignore the fact that five-year-olds don't always have the best, you know, *aim*.

Plus, the funky smell in the cabin has not dissipated. I think there must be something growing in the bilge.

Off to the store to buy Soft Scrub. With Bleach.

Island Time
Keeping calm
11:50 a.m., August 21

My mom and Finn are off on another "educational outing," and my dad is sitting in the bar at the Pickled Pirate, working on his book. With everyone out of the way, I decided this was a good opportunity to slay the bilge monster.

Like most sailboats, the floor of the *Island Time* is divided into panels, which can be pulled up for access to the bilge. Equipped with a scrub brush and keg of Mr. Clean, I slid the barrel bolt on the first panel and hefted it up. A fraction of a second later, I was scrambling up the companionway ladder, gasping for air. I collapsed on the deck, my eyes watering.

"Are you okay?"

With effort, I lifted my head and squinted at the blurry blob in front of me. I blinked a few times to clear the tears from my eyes. "Tess?" I asked wonderingly. Is bilge odor a hallucinogen?

"I caught a ride out here after yoga. Just to say hi. I hope that's okay?"

"Foul, foul stinky," I groaned. "Escape while you can."

"Well, I was kind of counting on you giving me a ride back to shore." She wandered over and stuck her head into the companionway. "Wooooo!" She yanked her head out quickly. "That *is* foul stinky!"

"Told ya."

"Well, what do you want to do about it?" she asked.

All the hatches were open, so we gave the boat a few minutes to air out, then ventured below.

"Here." I bravely handed her the Mr. Clean, keeping a bottle of generic brand for myself. "You take this."

She protested, "Caitlin, no, you should take th—"

I held up my hand. "I insist. It's awesome of you to help, but this isn't your fight. You take the Mr. Clean. I'll be fine."

We ran the bilge pump for a while to drain the fetid water, then poured fresh water and cleaner into the empty bilge and got to scrubbing. I won't lie; it was a horrific job. We attacked each section of bilge in turn, steadily making our way from the front of the boat to the back.

"Umm . . . Caitlin?" Tess asked, peering beneath the last floor panel. "Check this out."

Together we lifted out the panel and looked down into the compartment. I sat back on my heels, baffled.

"What is that?" I asked, eyeing the large, square package, securely wrapped in duct tape and black garbage bags.

"That," Tess said slowly, "is what they call a 'square grouper.'"

"There's fish in there?" That would certainly explain the smell.

"Noooo, they're called that because fishermen find them in the ocean sometimes. When drug shipments go astray."

"You mean . . ."

"Yup."

We both sat.

"You know," I mused, "Bertrand over at The Pickled Pirate thinks the old owners used this boat to smuggle cigars."

"Or something."

"Or something," I agreed.

"What are you gonna do with it?" Tess asked, looking serious for once.

I had no freaking idea. We stared at each other for long moments, both of us at a loss. Finally, I shook my head and shrugged. "Put the floorboards back?"

Tess bit her lip. "I think we need help."

The Pickled Pirate
Carrying on
1:30 p.m., August 21

Tess called Jonas, and Jonas called the twins. They met us at The Pickled Pirate, where we sat at a table near the bar and ordered all the nachos.

While we waited, I explained about the bilge bale.

"And then we put the floorboards back and called you guys," Tess added when I'd finished.

"Dear Lord. I didn't hear this," Bertrand said, hustling off toward the kitchen.

I glanced around the table. Enzo's jaw was slightly agape, and his eyebrows were two inches higher than normal. Jonas had his hand over his mouth. Lucas was the only one who didn't look concerned.

"Thisss," he breathed, "is legendary."

Tess smacked him with the back of her hand. "It is NOT legendary." She turned to Jonas and Enzo. "So that's why we called you two. We're trying to think of what to do next."

"What about me?" Lucas asked. "You called me, too."

"We called you because you love nachos," Tess said.

"Not a lie," he murmured.

"What we need," I told them, "is a plan to get rid of this stuff."

"Ummph." Lucas sounded pained. "Get rid of?"

"All right, look." Enzo placed his hands flat on the table. "This does not sound like a Caitlin-Tess-Enzo-and-Jonas problem."

"Hey!" Lucas objected.

Enzo ignored him and continued, "This sounds like an adult problem. And isn't that your dad, right over there?" He pointed to the table in a far corner of the restaurant where my dad, equipped with a laptop, noise-cancelling headphones, and coffee, was typing ponderously about snail fever or something.

"Like I can tell *him*!" I exclaimed. "He'd go straight to the police!"

Enzo looked at me askance. "Yehhhhs, that's what one typically does when they stumble across a fortune in illegal contraband."

So here's the thing: Onessa's thoughts on live-aboards the other day, calumnious and insulting as they may have been, are not unique to passive-aggressive mean girls. You see, live-aboards—as opposed to people who are just chartering sailboats for their vacations—are viewed with a certain amount of suspicion throughout the Caribbean. You might even say there's a stigma to it. It took my parents months and months just to get our visa. They had to submit bank statements and character references and all kinds of stuff. The BVI had not been all that excited to have us.

I laid it out plainly. "We are nonresident live-aboards. If my dad calls the police, they could revoke our cruising permit. Or our visas. They might even seize our boat." Or worse! And my mom just quit her job. We can't afford for my dad to go to prison. *Someone's* got to pay for my college.

No one took issue with my logic. Bertrand reappeared and

handed out waters, sodas, and dampening looks. We all sipped in silence until Enzo spoke again.

"Okay, okay. Tess, how about your dad takes it in to the police? Says he found it on the boat ramp or something. They're not throwing *him* out of the country. He's a Belonger."

Tess shook her head. "He won't do it. My auntie's in a fight with the commissioner's cousin."

"Oh. Hmm." He drummed his fingers on the table. "I guess our dad could take it in, but I was really hoping he wouldn't notice us for the rest of the summer."

"That would be best," Lucas concurred. "Wait, I know! Jonas can give it to his granny."

Jonas turned to Lucas with an appalled expression. "What's my granny want with it?!" he demanded.

"She can put it in that bush tea she's always making for everyone."

Jonas gave his head an incredulous shake. "Mehson . . ."

"Look," I said. "We don't need to turn it in." I glanced at Lucas. "Or *use* it. We just need to get rid of it. And not get caught."

"Well, it's too much to flush," Lucas said, pouting a little.

Everyone was quiet until, finally, Jonas offered, "I heard the Pockwood Pond incinerator is down."

Tess looked up hopefully. "They're burying trash on the hill again?"

Folks, we have a plan!

Ooh, and nachos.

Island Time
Faint with relief
4:20 p.m., August 21

After nachos, Tess and the boys headed home in a taxi (because their dad took the Range Rover to work today) and I headed back out to *Island Time* to vanquish the bilge monster, once and for all. I also need to repackage the bilge bale in something less conspicuous so we could set our plan in motion.

Bertrand mentioned he had a bag that might work for that (while still disclaiming all knowledge of what we were up to) and promised to send it out to me ASAP. I really have to hand it to Bertrand: not only does he make the tastiest cocktail garnish in the West Indies, he's also a super-handy guy to know in a crisis.

While I waited, I went below and wrestled the bale out of the bilge, which was easier than I'd anticipated due to its light weight. Then I poured the last of the Mr. Clean into the remaining section of bilge and set to scrubbing.

As I scrubbed, I reviewed the plan in my head, testing it for flaws. I found none. There's a beautiful simplicity to this plan. It's practically foolproof. It goes something like this:

I will conceal the bale in Bertrand's bag and, at the earliest opportunity, transport it to The Pickled Pirate, where I will temporarily stash it behind the chicken shed. Then, in a few days when the twins' house manager goes on vacation, they will borrow her car (because everyone on the island knows their dad's Range Rover), collect me and my bale from The Pickled Pirate, and convey us to Pockwood Pond. There, under cover of darkness, we will toss the bale into the open landfill and drive away, footloose and ganja-free. Easy-peasy lemon squeezy.

A knock on the hull interrupted my musings. I scrambled topside to greet Bertrand and almost tumbled back down the companionway when I instead found Tristan tying off a painter on the *Island Time*'s stern cleat.

"Tristan!" I gasped.

I'd fully expected him to write me off after the full moon disaster, so I was slow to process the reality of him, here, on my boat . . .

presumably to see me! It was like the clouds I had been living under parted and the sun finally came out. Not the actual sun—I'm no fan of that one, and it was currently burning down so hotly even my fingernails were sweating. No, I mean, a metaphorical sun. A golden, glorious orb of romantic enlightenment that gently warmed my insides without frying my nose.

I righted myself and tried to look calm as he approached.

"Hallo there." He gave me a rueful smile. "How are you?"

I almost couldn't answer, he looked so perfect. Better than perfect—splendid! The gods on Olympus should look so glorious. (No offense to Jesus. I'm sure he was pretty fit, too, but he usually doesn't look so good on those crosses.)

"Listen," I started, "about the party. I am *so* sorry."

He blinked.

"I had no idea there was rum in those drinks," I hurried to explain. "I would never have gulped them down like that if I'd kno—"

"Hey. *Hey.*" He held up a hand, halting my words. "It's okay."

That was so kind of him! But I'd made a fool of myself and ruined our evening, and let him pay for all my drinks, which were probably really expensive considering they were alcoholic.

"But I—"

He stopped me with a finger on my lips. "It's all forgotten."

"Can I at least pay—"

"Forgotten," he repeated firmly.

Intelligent, physically perfect, *and* gracious. Is he the most amazing guy in the world or what?

"Excellent," I sighed.

He leaned over and gave me a quick, warm kiss. "That's my girl."

He called me *his girl*! EEEEEEEEE.

"Now," he ordered, "tell me we're okay."

"We're *so* okay," I said, floating about ten inches above the deck.

"Great." He smiled brilliantly and took a seat in the cockpit. Taking my hand, he pulled me down beside him. "But, listen," he said, "there's a reason I came out here."

"Oh?" I asked. Then, "*Oh!* You've brought the bag! Or whatever Bertrand sent."

I scrambled aft and peered down into his dinghy. It looked familiar. "Is this Jonas's dinghy?" I asked.

"Oh, yeah, I borrowed it," he answered. In the bottom of the dinghy, I spotted a faded, black canvas duffle bag, the kind everyone uses to transport dive gear.

"This is the bag?" I asked. "The one I'm supposed to put the, umm, stuff in?"

Tristan blinked and gave me a big smile. "Yes. Yes, it is. Hope it's big enough."

It looked it. In fact, I thought I'd seen Jonas use it to carry around his turtle device, and that was maybe even a little bit bigger.

I tugged on the painter to pull the dinghy in closer, nabbed the bag, and handed it up to Tristan. Then, together, we went below, loaded the bale in the duffle, and zipped it closed.

"Perfect," I said. "Now I just have to find an opportunity to sneak it ashore and hide it."

"I can do that for you," Tristan immediately volunteered.

"Oh, no." I shook my head. "I can't ask you to do that. What if you got caught with it?"

He laughed. "I won't. Who would look twice at this?" He nudged the nondescript bag with his toe. "Honestly, it's fine." He leaned down and rested his forehead against mine. "I'm at your service."

Sa-woon.

"Well, I guess it *would* be easiest if you could take it now," I said. Then I wouldn't have to worry about sneaking in to shore without my parents noticing.

Tristan clapped his hands together. "Great! That's settled then."

Up on deck, Tristan gave me another quick kiss. Then he gave me a slightly longer one. And another. Breaking away, he said, "I should go." He rubbed the backs of his fingers against my cheek and promised, "Don't worry about any of this. I'll be in touch soon."

"Oh-okay," I promised, feeling kind of breathless.

That's one promise I'll have no trouble keeping; I have *much* better things to think about.

He tossed the duffle in the dinghy and cast off.

"Wait," I called out, "I forgot to tell you where to hide it! It needs to go behind the chicken shed."

Tristan gave me a thumbs up and started the engine.

"Thank you!" I yelled as he motored away.

I love it when a plan works out.

CHAPTER 11

Island Time
Productive but pining
6:13 p.m., August 22

Today, with the bale safely away from the boat, I got back to work. Restoring *Island Time* to its former glory is going to be a big, big job—although, looking at it now, it's hard to imagine its former glory was all that glorious.

Finn wandered up as I began sanding the teak trim that runs around the edge of the deck. "Look, Caitlin." He held up a grubby white blob. "I made you out of a cheese stick. I ate your entire body and now there's only your face left. I'm going to eat it slow and painful."

I ignored this.

After a moment, he finished his cheese and got bored. "Whatcha doing?"

"Sanding the toe rail."

"Why?"

"Because the varnish has peeled off and now it's all splintery."

"Can I help?"

I eased back for a moment and considered. The goal was to sand evenly until the toe rail was just barely sanded smooth. If I turned

Finn loose on it, he would sand like a bumper car and there would be spots sanded thin and spots sanded not at all. Then again, he probably wouldn't stick with it for very long. He's only five, after all.

And I wasn't sure why I was so worried about it. Even if I sanded and varnished expertly—which would be a neat trick considering I'd never done this before—this toe rail would never be perfect. It had clearly Been Through Some Things.

I shrugged and handed Finn my extra sanding block. "Here you go. Why don't you work on the other side, and we'll meet in the middle?"

As I'd predicted, Finn lost interest after eight minutes of furious sanding and went below to have a juice box, but I kept at it. As tasks go, it was hot, sweaty, and completely unrewarding—but it was something I could fix. I mean, sure, there were other things I could work on. The half-scraped hull taunted me, it looked SO BAD. But my shrimp trauma was too fresh.

Also, in the back of my mind lurked the hope Tristan might stop by again. He promised he'd be in touch. And if he happened to motor up, I wanted to be on deck to greet him. That way, he might not have to meet my mom.

But when, after three determined hours of sanding, I heard a dinghy nudge the hull, it wasn't Tristan who tossed me a line.

"Oh. Hi, Jonas," I said, wiping my hands on my shorts. Sweat and sawdust had mixed to form sticky sludge on my hands, arms, and knees. Maybe it was for the best Jonas had turned up instead of Tristan. Clad in my freak shirt and a floppy hat, positively *dripping* with dusty glop, I was probably as far from Tristan's idea of soulmate at that moment as I could get.

Jonas, on the other hand, didn't even seem to notice. "I saw you working and thought you might like a hand." He gestured to his turtle box. "I'm finished testing for the day."

Well, he was bound to be more help than Finn. "Sure," I said. "Thanks." I glanced down and surveyed the run of toe rail I'd been laboring over. It wasn't pretty.

"I don't think I'm doing this right," I said.

Jonas bent down to have a closer look. "I think there might be some rot there. You probably have to replace this."

"Great." I dropped my sanding block to the deck.

"Have you been at it long?"

I gave him a look that I hope conveyed my existential despair.

"Ah, okay, well," he said as he rubbed his neck, "maybe I'm wrong. Maybe we could save it."

I sighed in defeat. "No. You're right. I should have figured that out for myself."

He politely refrained from agreeing.

"Those are some pretty nasty gouges in the hull," he commented.

"Yep."

"Why don't we work on those? It's not good for rain to get in the hull, you know."

"I don't know how to work with fiberglass," I admitted. It was something I'd planned to google next time I was on Frenchman's Cay doing laundry.

"I can show you, if you want."

"You know how to do glass work?"

"Sure."

And so I spent the rest of the afternoon learning the venerable craft of fiberglass repair.

First, we zipped over to the chandlery for supplies. (Fortunately, my mom handed up her credit card, because that stuff was not cheap!) Then Jonas ducked into the dive shop while I had another go at the deli counter. The same woman from before watched as I approached. I hoped her meeting had gone well.

After waiting my turn, I asked politely, "Could I please have half a pound of sliced turkey?"

"No," she answered. "Turkey's finished."

"But"—I pointed to the case—"there's turkey right there."

"That turkey's not for sale."

"Well, when will there be turkey for selling?"

She only shrugged.

I left and met Jonas outside the dive store. "Let's get some sandwiches from Omar's."

Fiberglass repair turned out to be a lot of fun. Standing in Jonas's dinghy for easier access to the side of the hull, we added resin, fiberglass strands, and something Jonas called "bubbles" (which he explained was a colloidal thickener, like I'd know what that was, either) in a paper cup. Then he added a catalyst and stirred it all around with a pencil until it formed a peanut butter–like consistency.

"The resin sticks everything together," he explained, "and the catalyst makes it harden."

I leaned in to have a look and wrinkled my nose.

"Don't breathe it," he added.

Now he tells me. I know what happens to people who sniff things like that. Sam Giancarlo was in my study hall when I was in ninth grade and he was in eleventh. He spent most of the year sniffing model glue in the back of classroom and then got a combined score of 610 on the SATs. Now I hear he hangs out behind the Super Walmart in Glen Burnie huffing industrial lubricant and selling bootleg Pokémon cards to third graders.

Jonas smeared the mixture into one of the gouges and mushed it around until he was happy with the shape. Kind of like sculpting, but with noxious chemicals instead of Sculpey.

"When it hardens," he said, "we'll sand it smooth, spray some gelcoat over the top, and then we should be okay. Unless we need to fill it in more. Sometimes it sinks when it dries."

"What would happen to the resin if you didn't add the catalyst?" I asked.

"It wouldn't kick."

"Kick?"

He showed me the paper cup he'd used for mixing the resin. What little remained was hard as cement in the bottom of the cup, the pencil he'd used as a stirrer trapped there for eternity, like a dinosaur in a tar pit.

"So, if you didn't add the catalyst, the resin would be sticky, but it wouldn't 'kick'?"

"Right," he said, giving me a curious look.

I returned his look with a big smile. I had a plan.

The Pickled Pirate
Eating dinner
7:05 p.m., August 23

I spent today filling gouges with fiberglass, just like Jonas showed me. He promised to come back tomorrow and help me sand them all smooth.

Instead of my big, floppy hat, I wore a nice, streamlined sun visor while I worked. I won the sun visor playing trivia at Galway Bay, an Irish restaurant back home in Annapolis. The visor is navy blue and has a little shamrock embroidered on the front. It doesn't keep the sun off nearly as well as my ugly hat, but the overall look is hopefully more "keeper" than "beekeeper." I want to look my best in case Tristan stops by.

As it turned out, plenty of people stopped by today, but none of them were my one boy, one steady boy, one boy to be with forever and ever, one boyyyyyy, not two or three! (Sorry. Can't help myself. Great song.)

My first visitor was Tess, who stopped by after yoga again. She was willing enough to learn about fiberglass repair and spent an hour or so helping me patch holes. She also told me all her newest jokes, even though I begged her not to. There's really no such thing as free labor.

"Did it rain last night?" she asked, as I ferried her back to shore.

I glared at the water sloshing around in the bottom of the dinghy. "Nope."

It hasn't rained the whole time we've been down here. I think it's too hot to rain. The rain would boil and evaporate before it hit the ground.

It's probably a good thing *Island Time* has no sails. Knowing my mom, she'd want to take it out for a few nights at Norman Island or something, and between the holes in the hull and the leaky dinghy, I doubt any of us would make it back from that outing. Not without some help from Virgin Islands Search and Rescue.

My next visitors were not nearly as helpful as Tess.

I was sitting on the back of the boat, filling a gouge in the stern platform, when a yellow fiberglass dinghy motored up carrying two white guys about my dad's age. This concerned me because my mom and Finn had gone off snorkeling again, and I was there all alone. But then one of the guys called, "Hey there," and I relaxed a little, thinking maybe they knew my dad from the bar at The Pickled Pirate or something.

In my defense, they both looked like the kind of guys who would hang out at The Pickled Pirate, although I think I would have noticed them because the restaurant isn't exactly crowded this time of year. This first guy was tall with short, thick, gray hair and a deep tan. He wore sunglasses, a flat-brimmed cap, and a T-shirt that said

"Rollin' With My Gnomies." His friend was slimmer with a shiny bald head and a loud Hawaiian shirt.

"Hi," I said. "Are you looking for my dad? Because he's working."

"Well, that's cool, 'cause we don't actually need your dad for this," said Gray Hair. They drifted closer, and I noted the bald guy's Hawaiian shirt featured purple mermaids clad only in Viking helmets driving lime-green golf carts. Mmkay.

"Why?" I asked, still staring at the shirt.

"This used to be our boat. We forgot something," said Gray Hair. "We just need to step aboard for a sec and get it."

"You forgot something," I repeated, confused.

Both men gave me meaningful looks.

I failed to catch any meaning. "What did you forget?" I asked warily. "If it's the cooler you want, you can't have it. My mom's using it to store her sourdough starter."

"You can keep the cooler. That's not what we want."

"Then what?" I asked.

Gray Hair sighed. "We want, you know," he said significantly, "our *stuff*. Under the *floorboards*."

"O-oh," I said, finally getting it. "*That* stuff." I nodded. They nodded. "Well, it's not here anymore."

They quit nodding.

"What do you mean it's not there anymore?"

I shrugged nervously. "Well, we—I—" Probably best to leave the others out of this. "—moved it. So I could clean the bilge. And I thought I should, you know, get it off the boat."

The bald guy kicked the side of their dinghy and used several words that were new even to me. (I did not write them down. They weren't the kind of words you find on SAT vocab lists.)

"Okay," said Gray Hair, taking a visibly perturbed breath, "why don't you tell us where our stuff is *now*."

"Hey!" I cried, as Bald Guy's hand whipped out and grabbed my arm.

He gave me a shake. "WHERE'S OUR STUFF, LITTLE GIRL?"

"Behind the chicken shed!" I cried. "Go! Go get it! I don't want it!"

"We will"—Gray Hair's hands landed on my shoulders—"and you're coming with us."

Okay, this development was unexpected, but as I thought it through, I realized these guys turning up to reclaim their contraband was a lucky break. The bale would be off our hands, and the twins and I could scrap our fieldtrip to the landfill. (Ha—see what I did there? Scrap. LOL.)

We piled in their dinghy and motored off in the direction of The Pickled Pirate, Gray Hair at the helm.

"So did you guys notice my fiberglass work?" I asked, making small talk. "I fixed a lot of stuff."

Bald Guy gave me a derisive look. "Looked sloppy to me."

Uh! "Well, good thing the boat came with so many holes for me to practice on," I said indignantly.

Gray Hair glared. "It's a boat. It bumps into things."

"Boats don't just 'bump into things,'" I told him. "Haven't you ever heard of fenders? You guys must have hit every dock between here and Venezuela."

Neither of them commented.

I studied some odd spots on Bald Guy's skin.

"You should google the symptoms of scurvy," I advised.

"You should shut up now," he growled.

I took his advice and gave myself a little pep talk as we approached the dinghy dock. All I had to do was show these guys their stuff and I'd be rid of them forever. Nothing to worry about.

Five minutes later, we stared at the empty space behind the chicken shed, and I decided to worry.

"Where is it?" Bald Guy demanded.

I held up my hands. "I don't know. It was supposed to be here! Maybe—maybe it's *in* the shed!"

But the stuff wasn't inside the chicken shed, either. We checked the equipment shed as well, and the housekeeping closet.

"We are not messing around with you, kid," Gray Hair said in a hard voice.

"Look, I need to call my friend," I said. "He must have misunderstood and stashed it in the wrong place."

Bald Guy grabbed my arm again and pulled me close. My vision filled with teeth. "We'll be back tomorrow," he said in a menacing tone.

"Well, we've got that thing . . ." Gray Hair interjected.

"We'll be back in three days," Bald Guy amended. "You better have our stuff by then, or we're going to be really unhappy."

That makes three of us.

CHAPTER 12

The Pickled Pirate
Stress-eating breakfast
7:10 a.m., August 24

First thing this morning, I dinghied in to The Pickled Pirate and used their phone to call Tess. I'm no criminal mastermind but I've seen enough legal thrillers to know this wasn't the kind of thing we should be texting about.

Tess answered on the fourth ring. "Eh?"

"Tess? It's Caitlin. Listen, I hate to wake you up, but I really need to talk to your brother."

"Oo?"

"*Tristan*," I said, with a touch of impatience. "I need to talk to Tristan."

"Umph. Hold on." There was some scuffling and the sound of footsteps echoing through a house. A door opened and closed. Finally she said, "Not here."

What? "It's six thirty in the morning. He's already gone?"

"He probably hasn't come home yet."

"Hasn't come home yet? Home from where?!"

She gave a loud sigh. "Look, Caitlin, I don't know. This happens a lot."

"I . . . what?" My mind raced. "Never mind. Could you just text me his number?"

"Ummm . . ." Her voice grew fainter as she pulled the phone away from her face. "Ayyyyyyyy . . . don't have it. Sorry."

Why wouldn't she—*arrgh!* "Okay. Maybe you could get it from you mom? And text it to me? And please tell him when you see him that I need to talk to him? *Soon?*"

"Caitlin, what's going on? What's wrong?"

I paused. Tess already knew about the "stuff," but I couldn't see dragging her into my problems with Gray Hair and Bald Guy. She's my friend, and friends don't involve friends in conflicts with drug runners.

"Caitlin?"

But! What if the twins borrowed a car early and dealt with the bale without telling me? They wouldn't have been able to call me about the change of plan because they didn't have my number. OMG, WHAT IF THE BALE WAS ALREADY IN THE LANDFILL!

"Caitlin!"

"Tess. I think . . . I think our plan might have a wrinkle."

Tess, it seemed, was not a student of legal thrillers. Two minutes later, she had looped everyone into a group chat, and it was blowing up.

> Lucas: i swear we didn't take it!
>
> Enzo: we rly did not
>
> Lucas: does this mean we don't get to go to the dump
>
> Jonas: how long before they come back
>
> Tess: 3 days ☹💀
>
> Me: Please don't use the dead emoji

I clicked the screen off, feeling very unhappy, and ordered some breakfast.

Island Time
Plotting and packing
3:36 p.m., August 24

I don't know, Erica. I think you better get the turkey yourself," I confessed.

"You're being silly."

"I'm not. I haven't been having great luck with that."

She shook her head. "Caitlin, you have to *let go*. Discovering the rhythm of island life is just a matter of slowing down and opening yourself to the pace of nature. Look how well Finn's adjusting!"

I glanced down at the floor of the salon, where my brother lay nibbling tiny strips off the Fruit Roll-Up that he'd wrapped around his Spiderman action figure.

Finn looked over and caught us watching. "I'm eating his skin," he announced.

"Yeah," I said to my mom. "That's one well-adjusted kid you got there."

She sighed. "Fine. Finny? Do you want to come with me to the market?"

He did not. My mom grabbed her purse and sloshed off in the dinghy to buy turkey. I made Finn a sandwich with our last three slices of cold cuts and left him gnawing on Spidey while I changed into my Speedo tank suit. Over my Speedo, I layered my longest board shorts and a high-neck, long-sleeved rash guard. I checked myself out in the mirror. Only the skin of my face, hands, calves, and feet was visible. Good for sun protection, but it wasn't the sun I was worried about.

Up on deck, I pulled my snorkeling gear out of the aft lazarette locker and climbed down onto the stern platform.

It was a nice day. The ocean was calm, and the air was a degree or two less sweltering than usual. Looking out of the harbor, the next few islands in the chain—Peter Island, Norman Island, and, to the right, St. John—were a distinct and vibrant green in the clear, bright air. The smell of salt and fiberglass teased my nose. Water lapped against the hull, a pure, sparkling wash of crystalline blue that *begged* me to dive in. I sat on the stern platform, my feet dangling in the water, and tried not to wonder if I would soon be the victim of a drug-related murder.

I was still sitting there ten minutes later when Jonas dinghied up alongside.

He'd texted earlier that he'd be down working on his turtle box, and when I told him I planned to have another go at the barnacles, he offered to help.

"You still want to do this?" he asked.

"Well," I said, staring down at the water, "I can't leave it like this."

"Sure, you can."

And leave a half-scraped hull as my legacy? I don't think so!

"I could," I acknowledged—calmly, because I'm New Caitlin—but, then, because these could be my final hours, I added honestly, "but it would bug me."

"We could sand all those fiberglass patches instead," he offered.

"I already did." Sleep had not come easily last night (being threatened by smugglers will do that to you). And they say you shouldn't stay in bed when you're suffering from insomnia. I'd had to do *something* to pass the time.

"Okay, then." Jonas shrugged out of his shirt. "I'll help. Got a mask I can borrow?"

A cute guy just shucked his shirt in front of me. I *had* to check him out—the compulsion is encoded in my DNA. So I couldn't help but notice that Jonas has a very nice chest. Not as nice as Tristan's, of course. Tristan's chest is a masterpiece of lithe muscularity, whereas Jonas's is much . . . thicker. All those bulky muscles just aren't to my taste.

Really.

I hurried below and grabbed the mesh bag that holds my dad's snorkeling gear, along with Finn and a handful of Power Rangers to keep him occupied.

"Hang out up here and eat your sandwich," I told him, depositing him and his toys in the cockpit. "If you need to go below for anything, let me know first."

"What kind of sandwich is this?" Finn asked.

"Ham."

"I don't like ham."

"Well, until Erica gets back with more turkey, it's all we've got."

"I don't like ham," he repeated, his brows descending.

Ugh. I had real problems in my life. I just couldn't with the devil toddler right now. "Fine," I told him. "Starve."

On the stern platform, Jonas had already pulled on my dad's mask and fins.

"Ready?" he asked.

"Ready," I pronounced bravely. And in we jumped.

This time, the barnacle-scraping went much better—at least in one respect. Jonas demonstrated how scraping the hull while treading water *up*-current sends most of the shrimp floating harmlessly away. We fell into an efficient rhythm, scraping and chipping and scrubbing. Intrigued by the noise, Finn wandered over to the rail to watch as we worked. Between the two of us, the remaining side of the *Island Time* was clean in no time. I went back over some particularly tough spots, while Jonas free-dove down to scrape what he could of the rudder and keel. The fourth time he came up for air, he appeared beside my shoulder and spit out his snorkel.

"Swim around to the stern and get out of the water," he said calmly.

"What?"

"I think we should get out of the water."

I met his eyes, which usually sparkled with humor even when he wasn't laughing. Now they looked wide and very serious behind the glass of the dive mask.

"Okay," I said, a little freaked out.

I made for the stern platform but stopped and turned when I felt him tug on my fin.

"Slow," he said.

I resumed swimming, slowly, but considerably more freaked out than before.

When both of us were out of the water, I pulled off my mask. "What was that all about?"

"Come on," he said, removing his fins, "I'll show you."

I followed him up onto the deck and over to *Island Time*'s port side. We leaned against the lifelines and looked down into the water. Sticking out from under the boat was a large tail.

"What the—" I started.

"Come on," he said again, leading me across the boat to the starboard rail. Together, we looked over the side.

I repeated one of the words I'd learned from the smugglers.

"Yeah," Jonas agreed.

Emerging from beneath this side of the boat was a gigantic fish head.

"Is that a barracuda?" I asked.

"A really big barracuda," he confirmed.

I took another peek over the rail. A really toothy barracuda.

"So," I said, "if the head's over here, and the tail's sticking out over there, then it must be . . ." I broke off, trying to judge the distance.

"Big," he finished for me.

Holy shrimp—understatement!

"They don't usually bite people," he said, "but this one's so big . . . I thought, better to be safe."

I nodded vigorously. "Safe is good." I thought for a minute, then asked, "So . . . why do you think it's hanging around here?"

"I don't know. They're territorial. I usually see them around the reefs. I don't know why this one would be under the boat," he hesitated, "unless someone's feeding it."

We both turned to look at Finn, who sat in the middle of the cockpit playing quietly with his red Paw Patrol pup.

"How was that sandwich, Finn?" I asked.

He blinked innocently. "Good."

"Did you eat it all by yourself?"

He got up and joined us at the rail. "Ooh, look at *that* fishy," he said, with unconvincing surprise.

"Did you feed anything to that fishy?"

Finn's tiny mouth stretched in a wide yawn. "I think I'll take a nap," he said. And went below.

Of course, I can't *prove* Finn was chumming the water with lunchmeat . . . but I do know that when my mom got back from the store, he asked her very sweetly to make him a turkey sandwich. Two sandwiches is a lot of food for a five-year-old.

I turned to Jonas once Finn was out of sight. "I am *so* sorry. I don't know what to tell you. My mom won't let me call an exorcist."

Jonas's eyes were once again sparkling. "It's fine. We're alive."

"No one's safe," I moaned.

He smiled. "Don't worry about it."

"Look, do you want a Coke or something? Maybe a fruit snack? I owe you for all the help. And, you know—the warning."

"I'm good," he assured me, still smiling. "But I should go. I promised to go by my granny."

I walked him aft and untied his painter for him while he climbed in his dinghy.

"Hey," he said, like he'd just remembered, "have you heard about the Last Bash?"

Last Bash? Oh, right, that thing Onessa and Viv were taunting me about.

"Sort of. What is it, exactly?"

"Just something we do before school starts. Every year, we take a bunch of boats up to North Sound and spend the night there. Hang out on the beach. Kiteboard. That kind of thing."

A party that lasts for days? Wow, my own personal hell! "Wow," I said, "that sounds awesome."

He nodded. "I'm going with the twins. Their dad is letting them take his boat, and there's plenty of room if you want to come."

"Umm . . ."

"Tess is coming, too, and I'm bringing the food." When I still hesitated, he added, "It might be a good thing for you to be somewhere else for a couple of days. In case those guys come back."

Hmm. That *was* a compelling point. But I can't see my parents agreeing to let me take off with a bunch of other teenagers for what essentially sounds like a forty-eight-hour beach party. Especially after the full moon fiasco.

On the other hand, this was exactly the sort of event New Caitlin would attend with gusto. Besides, what had Jonas said? "Everyone" goes. And "everyone" would surely include Tristan. I *yearn* to see him again. And I really need to ask him if he might *possibly* have somehow misplaced the missing bale? And, yes, avoiding angry drug smugglers sounds nice, too.

My powers of persuasion are great. Surely I can talk my parents around.

I took a deep breath. "When do we leave?"

Island Time
Teetering on the brink of ruination
9:11 p.m., August 24

C an you believe it? They won't let me go!

"*You're* the ones who kidnapped me to the Caribbean. *You're* the ones who said it'd be such a great experience. And now that I'm here, you're not even letting me experience it. You're not parents, you're a press gang!"

"Press gang?" My dad gave me a sardonic look. "What have you been reading?"

I know what I'm talking about. A press gang snatched Blade the Buccaneer off the streets of Bristol when he was just a lad of fourteen. He spent eight hellish years in the Royal Navy, which is why he now patrols the seas, exercising his vendetta against any vessel that sails beneath the Union Jack. Well, he used to, anyway, before Persephone quelled his raging soul with her tender touch.

"But look." I showed him a text Lucas had sent out on the group chat. "There's going to be an adult there. The boat manager is coming."

"No," my dad said.

"How can you not let me go?!" I demanded.

"Get a grip, Caitlin," my dad said. "There's no way."

Excuse me, but there is *always* a way. I just have to find it.

But this isn't even the worst of my problems. I texted Tristan's number four times today, and even called and left a detailed voicemail (Cost: $8), but he never responded. I called Tess again, who confirmed she'd given me the right number and promised to tell him to call me if she saw him.

I even skipped dinner at The Pickled Pirate on the off chance he might stop by the boat. But he never did.

And I've only got two more days until the smugglers come back for their "stuff." Unless they're counting from yesterday, in which case they might come back . . . tomorrow! No, they have to give me three whole days. Today. Tomorrow. The next day. And then they come back early on the fourth day to collect. That makes sense, right?

But what if they come back before I can talk to Tristan? I've *got* to get their stuff back for them or . . . or . . .

Or what?

Island Time
Packing, quick quick quick!
9:15 a.m., August 25

You want to know how I *know* there's a God? (Besides the decade-plus of Catholic indoctrination I've undergone?) Because of what happened this morning, that's how.

My parents and I were sitting around making instant coffee with water my dad boiled on the barbeque when we heard a funny noise. At first, I thought it was the buzz of an outboard engine, but when it didn't fade or get louder, we realized it was coming from somewhere on the boat.

"Finn, turn that off for a sec," my dad said.

But Finn, who was watching *Lightyear* on his iPad (okay, I might have been watching, too), ignored him.

"Finn, I need to hear what that noise is. Pause the movie," my dad said again.

Finn didn't so much as glance in his direction.

At this point, my dad reached over and hit the power button on the side of the iPad. The screen blipped off, but the ambient noise surged due to all the outraged screaming.

"Good going, Matt," I congratulated, "you should be able to track that noise down now, no problem."

I don't think he could hear me, though, not with his hands over his ears.

My mom calmly got up and pulled Finn's Spiderman headphones out of his little backpack. She paired them with his iPad, eased them onto his evil, orange head, and turned the movie back on.

Abruptly there was perfect silence. Well, except for the continuous whining buzz coming from somewhere on the boat.

My dad got up and examined the instrument panel. "The light's on for the bilge pump," he said.

"Switch it off," my mom suggested.

He shot her an exasperated look. "The bilge pump turns itself on for a reason. Namely to keep the boat from sinking."

"You think there's water in the bilge?" I asked doubtfully. After all, I scrubbed out that bilge just a few days ago, and it was mostly dry when I finished.

"Only one way to find out."

My mom, Finn, and I remained on the settee while my dad unbolted the closest floor panel and lifted it out.

"Hmm," my dad said.

"That's a lot of water," my mom said.

"Yeah, but look how clean it is down there," I said.

Forty minutes later, a guy from the marina hunkered over our bilge and offered his opinion.

"Looks like one of your through-hulls popped out. They can

corrode and come loose in these older boats. See, that's your depth transducer right there."

"Which means?" my dad prompted.

"There's a hole in the bottom of your boat."

"Does that mean we could *sink*?" my mom asked.

"Oh, sure." The guy nodded eagerly. "If your battery dies, the bilge pump will quit, and the boat will fill up with water."

My mom gaped.

"Okay, okay," said my dad, "How do we make sure the boat *doesn't* sink?"

"Well, for now, you can just do this." The guy reached into the bilge and pushed the depth transducer back into place. "You'll want to replace that with one that's not corroded as soon as you can get one," he advised, "and in the meantime, keep that battery charged so the bilge pump's got power. It could come loose again. And you might want to have your other through-hulls checked out."

"Things are *popping out* of the bottom of our boat?" my mom wheezed, her hand splayed across her chest.

"Oh yeah," the guy said.

Which is why we're moving back to The Pickled Pirate for the night while the marina guy lines up someone to check our hull for holes. Well, I should say *my parents and Finn* are moving back to The Pickled Pirate for the night. Because while my dad was griping about the cost of shoes and ships and ceiling wax (and marine surveyors) I stepped up with a helpful, cost-saving suggestion.

"If you let me go to the Last Bash, you'll only have to pay for one hotel room," I pointed out. "I'm sure they'd move a cot into your room for Finn to sleep on."

My dad fixed me with a hard stare.

I piled on a few more assurances. "I won't drink alcohol, I swear.

And I'll text you all the time. And I'll wear my hat. I won't talk to strangers. I won't stare directly at the sun—"

"You know what, Caitlin?" he said, looking hassled. "Fine. Go. I can't take any more aggravation today."

Yay!

CHAPTER 13

Aboard *Xanadu*
Free to be (the New) me!
11:20 a.m., August 25

At eleven, Jonas collected me from The Pickled Pirate, and to-gether we dinghied across to the marina, where the twins' dad keeps his boat. I guess I'd been expecting another sailboat, since that marina is full of them, but *Xanadu* is a big, shiny cabin cruiser with a fly bridge and tons of nifty amenities. There's even a giant TV and a wet bar in the cockpit.

Lucas, Enzo, and a deeply tanned white guy in a navy-blue polo were already aboard when we stepped off the dock. Music blared from the onboard speakers, and Enzo was wrapping twinkle lights around the stainless-steel railing. The foredeck was loaded down with watersports gear.

"Ahoy," Enzo called out, "and welcome aboard! Caitlin, this is Paul. He's the slip sergeant of this mighty gin palace. Sadly, he's unloaded all the gin for our present adventure."

"Nice to meet you," I said.

Paul gave a disinterested grunt.

"All right," Lucas announced, rubbing his hands together, "that's everyone. Ready to go?"

Paul took the helm, started the engines, and grunted at the twins, who cast off the dock lines and hauled in the fenders. He backed the boat out of the slip and motored around to the end of the dock, where he idled in place for a moment as he handed the wheel off to Enzo. Then Paul hopped off the boat and onto the dock.

"Umm." I pointed at Paul's retreating back. "Where is Paul going?"

"He's done now. He's our harbor pilot," Lucas explained. "Our dad won't let us move the boat around the marina unsupervised. We hit something once."

Somehow, I didn't think my dad's idea of supervision aligned with their dad's idea of supervision. I was clutching indecisively at my phone when Tess emerged from the cabin.

"Okay, I got another one: what do you call a cow with no legs? Anyone? Anyone? *Ground* beef!" She collapsed in a fit of honking giggles.

"That's not okay," I said, grinning reluctantly.

"Yay, you're here!"

Enzo looked to the sky. "Tell me why we invited her again?"

Lucas answered. "*I* said, 'I've almost forgotten how annoying Tess is,' then *you* said, 'Better have her along so she can remind us.' So, Tess, direct all your riddles to this young man right here." He slapped his brother on the back.

Enzo slapped him back.

Lucas gave Enzo a shove.

Enzo shoved Lucas, bracing himself against the steering station and putting a little more back into it. Lucas crashed into the beverage cooler.

"Umm . . ." I decided to interrupt before someone went over the side. "So how long will it take us to get there?"

"An hour, tops," Lucas answered.

"This is a very fast toy," Enzo added.

That was an understatement. We charged out of Soper's Hole to the throaty roar of twin diesels and, within minutes, were flying up the Sir Francis Drake Channel, bracketed by Tortola's coastline on the left and a series of smaller islands—Norman, Peter, Salt, Cooper, and Ginger—on the right.

For the first bit, I sat with Tess on the bow, our hair whipping about our heads as Tess laughed into the wind. Out in the channel, the breeze was refreshingly cool. Every now and then, the boat would plow into a wave, and a fine spray of white water would mist our legs, arms, and faces. At one point, we spotted a sea turtle as it surfaced for air on a nearby swell. Its enormous, rippled shell was dark and glossy in the bright sunshine. I watched, fascinated, as it scuttled rapidly back to the depths. I had no idea turtles were fast! It was easy to see why Jonas was so intent on saving them; they really were magnificent. I kept my eyes peeled, hoping to spot another, but after about twenty minutes of this, I started to feel a little sunburned and made my way aft to find some shade.

Jonas was stretched out across one of the padded bench seats reading a book on magnetic fields.

"Cold drinks in the cooler," he said, as I settled on the bench beside him.

I helped myself to a bottle of water and wondered how my parents and Finn were doing back at The Pickled Pirate. So, okay, leaving them alone to deal with Finn and our sinking sailboat? Maybe not my best moment. And I inadvertently lied about the adult supervision thing, although I suppose the twins are *technically* adults. Unhinged, but legally of age. But I really do think a change of venue is the wisest course of action for me right now—at least until I figure out what happened to that bale. And to do that, I really need to talk to Tristan and see if he maybe left the drugs behind some *other* chicken shed. And, according to Tess, Tristan will definitely be in North Sound for the Last Bash.

I wonder why he hasn't called or stopped by. I checked with Tess, but she says, as far as she knows, he hasn't been hospitalized or arrested or anything. I know he offered to help, but now that he's had time to think about it, I hope he's not mad I asked him to transport drugs . . .

Aboard *Xanadu*
Moored in North Sound!
1:34 p.m., August 25

We're here!

There was only one boat at anchor when we arrived in North Sound, a wide body of water at the northwest end of Virgin Gorda (third largest of the British Virgin Islands, second most populous, according to my guidebook). A smattering of smaller islands ringed the sound, forming a large, protected expanse of water. A few different resorts were visible, two on more distant shores and one right in front of us. We motored over to a mooring field in front of a resort and marina called Leverick Bay and picked up a ball.

"That's Moskito Island, and Prickly Pear, and Eustacia, and Saba Rock." Tess pointed to each island in turn. "And that one over there is Necker Island. It's got lemurs!"

I paid careful attention as she pointed out this last island, not because of the lemurs (although I wouldn't mind seeing some lemurs) but because I've heard it's regularly rented by A-list celebrities. Shelby would stroke out if I sent her a pic of Barack Obama sipping on a piña colada in a pineapple, or Harry Styles doing belly flops off a boulder.

One whole shore of the sound belongs to a small resort called the Bitter End, and there's a big sandy beach with a beach bar on it called Vixen Point located across from Leverick Bay. In the middle of the far pass, a postage stamp of an island called Saba Rock is entirely covered by another resort (creatively named Saba Rock), and Jonas says there are a few other places we can't see from our mooring. It doesn't really matter because all of these places are closed until October, which is why we're moored in Leverick Bay. Scattered on the hill above us is a neighborhood of colorful villas, so the resort here stays open year-round. Ashore I can see a restaurant, a palapa bar, and something that looks like a beached pirate ship.

I bet it's all quite lively during tourist season, but looking at it now, that's hard to imagine.

When I said so to Enzo, he shrugged. "Not many tourists around in August—only hurricanes. No sense in keeping everything open when there's no one around to use it."

"Besides," Lucas chimed in, "this way there's no one around to complain when a bunch of depraved teenagers descend on the place."

An excellent point.

The twins made their way to the bow and began unlashing watersports gear, while Jonas disappeared into the small but fancy galley (like, so fancy that not only does it have a stove, it has a *microwave*) to get lunch. Now, in my family, "lunch" means slapping some turkey between a couple of slices of whole wheat and maybe peeling an orange. But Jonas emerged from the galley with an aluminum roasting pan of barbecued ribs, another of corn on the cob, and a bakery box of round, fried pastries he called johnny cakes. Everyone immediately converged on the johnny cakes and I took a hasty step back.

"You can't have three!" Enzo slapped at his brother's hand.

Lucas turned to him with a johnny cake in each hand and one in his mouth and literally growled. I took another step back.

Jonas reached past them and handed me a plate already piled with ribs, corn, and johnny cake, and gave me a reassuring smile.

I'd just opened my mouth to thank him when Enzo let out a bloodcurdling scream. Tess and Lucas jumped, Jonas put his hand to his chest, and I nearly dropped my plate. Enzo calmly put his johnny cakes down on his own plate and said, "I better get that, it's probably Mum."

He moved toward the cabin as the bloodcurdling scream came again.

"Oh my god, Enzo," Tess exclaimed, "you promised you would change your ring tone!"

"I forgot," Enzo yelled back. He cut himself off mid-scream and said into the phone, "Hello, it is I, Enzo."

Tess held up her hands. "Why is he like this?"

"I can't explain it," Lucas said. "We were raised in the same house by the same parents and *I'm* perfectly normal."

We all stared at him.

"What?" he asked.

And as we all sat at the table, gnawing on ribs and attempting to cure Lucas of his delusion that he is a normal person, I realized—I mean, I don't want to presume, but it kind of *seems* like these people . . . like me? All four of them! That's three more people than I have ever voluntarily spent time with outside of school. And I'm having *fun*. Operation: Not A Freak is working!

Plus, I have found my destiny, my soulmate, who is brilliant and gallant and a fabulous kisser. Really, what more could I want? (Other than for Tristan to answer my texts. Soon!)

It's official: the old Caitlin is out; New Caitlin is in.

This year is going to slap!

Aboard *Xanadu*
Felt cute, had to retreat
2:05 p.m., August 25

While we were busy nomming, a small flotilla of boats flooded through the pass and into North Sound. Most picked up moorings around us in Leverick Bay, and the rest dropped hooks off Vixen Point. By the time we finished cleaning up lunch, the mooring field was packed and new arrivals began rafting up to other boats.

"Wow. All these kids go to St. Hilda's and St. Hugh's?" I marveled.

Enzo shook his head. "Boats come from St. John and St. Thomas and even Puerto Rico. Just wait until everyone gets here. You haven't seen anything yet!"

I stared out over the rollicking anchorage. "Oh," I said faintly. "Great."

People began diving off boats and swimming in to shore. Someone appeared on a jet ski. Those who'd come in boats big enough to pull dinghies motored in with coolers and speakers, and pretty soon the scene on the beach looked ominously like Sandy Point on the Fourth of July. (And if you've ever seen ten thousand Marylanders crammed onto a gravelly beach beside a tea-colored bay, you'll understand my lack of enthusiasm for going "downy ocean.")

Still, it's better than being murdered by drug smugglers!

"Everyone ready to play?" Lucas asked.

"Yessss." Enzo threw off his T-shirt. "Let's kite!"

"Sounds good," Jonas agreed. The boys pulled out bags of kite gear and started untangling leads.

Tess nudged my shoulder. "I'm going to hike up to Gorda Peak and take some photos. Want to come? It's an easy hike, you can do it in flip-flops. And the view is AMAYYYYYZINNNNG."

"Sure," I said. I don't know how to kiteboard and, New Caitlin or not, the beach scene looked nightmarish.

"Great! We can paddle the stand-up boards into the beach and get a taxi up to the trailhead."

I changed into my trusty Speedo, topped it with my adorable new beach cover-up, and we paddled in. Pulling our boards up high on the beach, we walked through the resort area to the parking lot and sat on a low wall, where Tess said we could wait for a taxi.

Apparently, it was a slow day for taxis. We watched people come and go from the resort, shoppers leaving with groceries, and staff arriving for the afternoon restaurant shift. A small group of white people in spandex cycling attire marched up from the dock carrying road bikes. I tilted my head as a tall man with a luxuriant mane of white hair mounted up and cycled by us, a lemur perched on his shoulder.

I pointed after them. "Was that . . .?"

"Uh-huh," Tess confirmed.

I turned to her with wide eyes.

"Virgin Gorda," she explained with a shrug.

Okey-dokey.

I pulled a tube of sunscreen from my daypack and started reapplying lotion to my arms. I held the tube out to Tess. "Do you need any?" I offered. "I brought three different kinds."

"Goat!"

"Well," I chuckled modestly, "I don't know about 'greatest of all time,' but I do like to be prepared. Sometimes you want the long-lasting coverage of an all-mineral sunscreen—I mean, this stuff is SPF-forever—but sometimes you just want a spray for fast application. And I also have a stick—"

"No. I mean there's a *goat*. Eating your cover-up."

"What?" I wheeled around and found myself hip-to-face with a large, brown goat, lurking just on the other side of the low wall. It had large, curved horns, beady, brown eyes, and a mouth filled with my skirt.

"Ahhhh!"

I sprang off the wall in a panic, which did not appear to disturb the goat at all. Stretching his neck to bridge the distance, he kept his mouth securely clamped around my cover-up and munched furiously.

"Let go!" I yelled in outrage. I grabbed the skirt (Cost: $86!!) at the waist and yanked. The goat yanked back. Tess reached over and added her muscle to the mix and, with a loud *riiiiiiiiip*, the skirt separated.

"*Maaaaaaaah,*" the goat bleated triumphantly, half my skirt dangling from his mouth, and bounded off up the hill.

Tess and I both turned to stare at the back of my now butt-less cover-up.

"You might want to go change," she suggested, just as I said, "You go on without me."

Aboard *Xanadu*
Third time's the charm
2:05 p.m., August 25

I slunk back to the boat, careful to keep my face to the world. I'd hoped to avoid any witnesses, but Jonas emerged from the cabin as I climbed aboard.

"I thought you went kiting," I said as casually as possible, careful to keep my back to the gunwale.

He gave me a curious look. "My cousin's friend is taking me out to a spot with lots of turtles. I'm going to do some testing. Want to come?"

I considered my other options. There weren't any. And Jonas was so nice and easy to spend time with. Plus, turtles. "Sure," I said.

I sidestepped into the cabin (which I'm sure did not seem weird *at all*) where I changed into shorts and a sunproof shirt. Not my most attractive look, but it's not like Jonas cared. We waited on deck until a small motorboat with a light blue hull pulled up.

Jonas slapped hands with the guy driving the boat and introduced him. "Caitlin, this is Plucky. He's the local turtle-whisperer."

Plucky was ready to go. "Let's do this! The grass bed in Oil Nut Bay has so many turtles, man. So many. Just got to stop by the island real quick and feed the lemurs."

"Yeah, yeah, no worries," Jonas told him. I helped Jonas transfer his turtle box to Plucky's boat, and off we went.

I stared curiously at the device as we motored across the sound to Necker Island. It was housed in a rigid black camera case, about the size of a small carry-on suitcase. On one of the panels, Jonas had installed binary on and off buttons, which he'd covered in a clear, plastic membrane for waterproofing.

"How does it work?" I asked him over the hum of the engine.

He looked *thrilled* that I'd asked. "Turtles have great magneto-reception," he explained. "They use the earth's magnetic field to navigate during migrations, and they use magnetic topography to develop magnetic maps of different areas. They're really sensitive. This device works by emitting a strong electromagnetic field—kind of like those Shark Banz that surfers wear to repel sharks."

"But yours repels turtles?"

"Ah . . ." He did a cute little head tip. "That's the idea. I haven't quite got the frequency right. Yet. But, once I do that, I'll work on scaling down the size so it can be attached to nets, which will help keep the turtles out of the bycatch."

Well, that was just . . . amazing. "So how are you going to test it?"

"I have a very precise and sophisticated method of trial." He shot me a sideways grin. "I drop it in the middle of a bunch of turtles and see if they swim away."

I made a fist. "Prepare to flee, turtles!"

"Welcome to Necker Island," Plucky announced as the blue boat pulled alongside a dock painted bright cherry red. The dock led to a sandy beach bordered by lush vegetation. In the distance, a large house sat on a tall hill. "You guys coming?"

Jonas shot me an inquiring look.

Did he really need to ask? "I want to see the lemurs!"

We followed Plucky across the island, past swanky, grass-rooved structures, tennis courts, and even an in-ground trampoline. We saw Aldabra tortoises the size of Suzukis and a salt pond filled with hundreds—maybe thousands—of extremely stinky flamingos. Finally, we reached a grove of palm trees enclosed by a tall fence. Plucky led us through a narrow gate and there they were. Big ones, small ones, fluffy ones, ring-tailed ones, each of them more adorable than the last with their big eyes and tiny person-hands. I believe I actually squeeed.

"Here." Plucky handed me a few hard, brown biscuits. "Show them the treats and they'll come to you."

Two minutes later, the lemur on my shoulder was delicately plucking lemur cookies, one at a time, from my outstretched palm, and I was as happy as I've ever been in my life. "I live here now," I announced.

Jonas, who had set his turtle device in the sand and was also covered in lemurs, murmured, "I live here with you."

"HEY!" Plucky yelled.

Jonas and I snapped out of our shared lemur trance to see Plucky sprawled on the ground by the gate, surrounded by a debris field of diced mango and lemur chow. Barreling past him were Gray Hair and Bald Guy, the erstwhile owners of *Island Time.*

I gasped in alarm. *How the heck had they found me here of all places?* The lemur on my shoulder snatched the last cookie from my hand and took off.

"I *told* you she had it," Bald Guy called over his shoulder to Gray Hair. He dashed across the lemur enclosure toward Jonas and snatched the turtle device up off the ground.

Now it was Jonas's turn to shout, "HEY!" He gently deposited his lemur on a nearby branch and charged toward Bald Guy.

Gray Hair held out a hand. "Back off, kid. We're here for our property."

"Wait, no!" I cried, racing toward them.

"What are you talking about? That is *mine.*" Jonas reached out, clasped the casing, and yanked. Bald Guy lurched forward but held on. I reached between them and attempted to peel Bald Guy's fingers from the plastic.

"THAT'S ENOUGH," Gray Hair yelled, brandishing a cartoonishly large, gun-shaped object at our heads. Jonas dropped his hands from the device and took a giant step back. Then he leaned forward again, grabbed my arm, and yanked me behind him.

"Is that . . . ?" I asked.

"Flare gun, yep," Jonas answered, his eyes huge.

The biggest flare gun I'd ever seen.

Bald Guy shot us a triumphant look and cradled the turtle box in his arms. "Glad we understand each other. We'll be taking this now."

"That's *not* your stuff," I exclaimed, peering around Jonas. "It's an experimental turtle-repulsion device."

Gray Hair pinned me with a sharp look. "Do we look like idiots?"

Jonas reached back and squeezed my arm before I could answer. "Look, man, she's telling the truth. It's just magnets and foam."

"Sure," Bald Guy said, "it just *happens* to be the same size and weight as our missing, ah, stuff."

"Open it and see for yourself," Jonas suggested in a very calm voice.

Gray Hair waved the hand not holding the flare gun at Bald Guy. "Open it," he ordered.

We all looked on as Bald Guy dropped the box to the sand and began hunting for the latches. He found the keypad instead. "It's some kind of safe," he announced.

Jonas shook his head, "No, it's not. Those are on/off buttons. The latches are on the other s—"

Gray Hair walked over and peered at the keypad. "What's the combination?" he demanded.

Jonas tried again. "The latches are right th—"

Gray Hair waved the flare gun around some more. "Give us the code!"

Jonas threw his hands up and said, "One-one-one-one."

"That's a terrible combination," Gray Hair commented. "What kind of cheap-o safe only has two numbers?"

Bald Guy reached out and hit the ON button four times. We waited several seconds and, predictably, nothing happened.

Jonas folded his hands behind his head and looked at the sky. "Now can I show you the latch—"

A lemur leapt through the air, landed on Bald Guy, and bit him on his shiny pate. "*Ahhhhhhhhh!*" he screamed.

Suddenly, the air was full of lemurs, leaping in from above and below to pile onto Gray Hair and Bald Guy (who now both were screaming).

Jonas grabbed my hand, and we sprinted for the gate.

I hesitated at the exit. "Your device . . ."

"Just *go!*" he yelled, pulling me through and slamming the gate behind us.

After that, Plucky took us straight back to the twins' boat. Needless to say, we didn't get to see any turtles (or try out the trampoline), but without Jonas's device, that would have been a pointless excursion anyway. Jonas was silent on the ride back and took off on a paddleboard as soon as we reached the *Xanadu*. I was sitting in the cockpit, trying to avoid further disaster, when a dinghy pulled up. I didn't recognize the kid driving, but Enzo sat in the bow.

"The party's moving to Vixen," he announced, pointing to the sandy point across the sound.

"Oh, okay, have fun," I told him.

"You're coming with us," Enzo declared.

"You know, this hasn't been a good day for me. I think maybe I'll just st—"

"No way. Get in. LET'S GOOOOOO!"

The very last thing I wanted to do—ever, but particularly at that moment—was party on a beach with my peers, but Enzo was insistent. And, having seen him in action, I was a little concerned he'd ban me from the boat if I continued to refuse. Also, there was a decent chance that Tristan would be over there. I was dying to see him, and if I didn't find out what happened to that bale, I might be just plain ol' dying.

"Alright, give me a minute," I said. I can't claim to be an expert on beach parties, but even I realized that New Caitlin could not show up to one in a sunproof shirt covered in lemur cookie crumbs. "I've gotta change into my suit." I grabbed my bag and ducked into the cabin, squeezed into the tiny head off the main salon, and locked the door behind me.

I'm not gonna lie, the loss of my bathing suit cover-up was a serious setback. But I had a contingency plan.

First, I set my bag on the lid of the toilet, stretched up on tiptoe, and unscrewed the knobs that secured the overhead hatch. This was going to require some ventilation. Then I changed into my bikini top and broke out the small can I bought yesterday at the marine supply store. Using a plastic knife, I pried the lid off the can and took shallow breaths, trying not to inhale too many resin fumes.

Wielding the knife with surgical precision, I spread thin trails of resin around the leg-holes of my bikini bottoms. I then wrapped the knife in a paper towel, pounded the lid back onto the can, and slowly, carefully eased my bikini bottoms over my feet. Stretching the fabric to keep the resin away from my skin, I slid the bottoms up my legs and over my butt before allowing them to snap into place.

There. One stay-put bikini, ready to party.

I know resin is probably not the best thing to smear all over delicate portions of anatomy, but it's not like I plan to make a habit of this. Once I cement my place in the social fabric, I'm sure I'll be able to work some board shorts into my wardrobe. Worst-case scenario, I'll just buy another cover-up. One that's goat-proof. But, for now, this is a perfectly workable solution. I left out the catalyst, so it's basically a harmless (if pungent) adhesive. Nothing to worry about. In fact, I should probably get an award for my ingenuity. Most Innovative Use of Marine Products, or something. That would look great on my college apps.

Okay. Here we go.

CHAPTER 14

Vixen Point
Demeaned and devastated
2:57 p.m., August 25

The moment we reached the dock, Enzo took off on a Jet Ski with someone, abandoning me to the tender mercies of strangers. I paused by the water's edge, stalling but also appreciating the stunning clarity of the water. It was just as described in that Gaelic Storm song my dad played nonstop after seeing them in concert at Rams Head last winter: gin clear. Like something out of a Brita commercial. And the sand was the palest of pale yellows, like whipped butter. I waded in and enjoyed until a little jerk of a bait fish gave my toe a sharp nibble, at which point I tamped down my rising social anxiety and slowly approached the crowd.

I *really* needed to find Tristan, but it's a nerve-wracking business, cruising up to a group of complete strangers. I've had plenty of nightmares that start that way. And in those nightmares, I usually wear clothes that offer more coverage than the skimpy yellow bikini. Underwear, for example. But, as soon as my feet hit the sand, a trio of girls wandered over and introduced themselves.

"Hi," said a curvy girl about my height with skin a few shades lighter than her dark brown hair. Her hair was smoothed back along her scalp into a tight ponytail and braided into a thick, dramatic braid. A small section of hair wrapped around the top, hiding the rubber band. "I'm Simone."

"I'm Leona," said her taller friend. Leona's hair was styled identically but colored a rich bronze that coordinated glamorously with her complexion.

I reached back and ran my fingers through my own hair in a futile attempt to detangle the limp, sweaty mess. I'm not jealous. You're jealous.

"Javonne," offered the third girl, whose bathing suit made my yellow bikini look like something Sister Philomena would wear.

"You must be Caitlin," Simone said.

My reputation preceded me? This New Caitlin thing was working out even better than I'd thought.

"Uh, yeah," I said, kind of startled by this development. "How'd you know?"

Simone laughed. "You're the only person here we don't already know."

Gotta love small towns—island chains—whatever.

And, as Simone dragged me around, introducing me to the crowd, I was further surprised by how enthusiastic everyone was. Like, *genuinely* excited. To meet ME!

"So *you're* Caitlin. Legendary!"

"It's an honor, lady."

"Always nice to meet a fellow consumer." (Wow, I'd never had anyone compliment my shopping skills before. See, I told you the yellow bikini is seriously cute.)

"You're my hero, man."

That last greeting was a little puzzling but still positive so, hey, I'll take it.

Honestly, at that point I was kicking myself for not attempting a personal reinvention years ago. By approaching social success like any other campaign, with study and a detailed plan of action, it was clear that popularity could be attained as easily as, say, State Math League Championship.

Of course, *maintaining* popularity comes with its own set of problems. And my problems started pretty quickly.

I accepted the can of Coke someone handed me and pretended to sip (Like I'm really going to drink Coke on a beach in the baking sun. Everyone knows caffeine is dehydrating!) but earned my first weird looks when I hesitated to take a puff of the cigarette they were circulating. I mean, I know smoking is still a thing in Europe, and this smelled like some kind of boutique brand, but even still . . . I took a closer look at the smoldering cancer stick Simone held out to me. It had a kind of DIY look to it . . .

Oh. Ohhh.

"No, no, that's okay," I said, hastily passing it along.

They all stared at me for long seconds, then a white guy, who'd said his name was Cameron—or maybe Colin?—laughed. "I get it, I get it. The soul of generosity."

I had no idea what he meant by that, but I attempted a gracious smile. There was a general shrug, and everyone went back to chatting.

"So what kind of music do you like?" Leona asked.

Oh, I was so ready for this. "I've been listening to lots of reggae since we moved here. Love Bob Marley!"

"Yeah, classic," she agreed. "Got a favorite song?"

"Um," I considered, "I really like 'Pixie Dust.'"

"What?"

"You know," I said, then sang a few bars—a thing I would not normally attempt, but it's a pretty easy tune. "'*Pixie dust! Movement of ja people.*'"

Leona opened her mouth but didn't say anything.

"I love the reference in that one. I'm a big Disney fan," I explained.

Everyone around us burst out laughing. And not the laughing-with-you kind of laughing. Believe me, I know the difference.

"Are you being serious?"

"This girl's a trip!" Cameron commented.

"She's kidding," said Simone. "You're kidding, right?"

"Oh, yeah." I laughed nervously. "Totally kidding."

Leona looked at me askance.

I sighed in relief when the conversation turned to some party scandal from the night before. But my relief was short-lived.

"I heard his parents were supposed to be in New York for another week."

"Yeah, and they told him after last year he couldn't have more than two people over at a time while they were gone."

"And when they came home, they found ten people skinny dipping in their pool."

"No, no. The best part was when Mr. Sidney went back inside and found Tristan and Angelika going at it under the pool table!"

I gasped. "Tristan?! As in *Tess's brother* Tristan?"

Javonne gave me a curious look. "Stepbrother. But yeah."

My heart just stopped. Literally, there was an enormous sucking feeling in my chest right where my heart is. Was. Like it disintegrated and left a bloody vacuum where that organ used to reside.

"It's not that big a deal," Simone chimed in, mistaking my existential anguish for something else entirely, "Mr. Sidney won't *do* anything about it. And I know Tristan didn't care." She paused. "Angelika might've."

"He's such a slut." Javonne laughed affectionately. "But I wish I'd seen the expression on Angelika's face."

I was going to cry. No, I couldn't. Not there, in front of everybody. That would be the end of New Caitlin, for sure.

"I've gotta go reapply my sunscreen," I said, as lightly as I could manage, "or I'm gonna fry."

"You can borrow mine," Javonne offered, holding out a bottle of SPF 15.

"Thanks," I said, and laughed a little desperately, "but until I get my base tan going, I need to stick to the strong stuff. Back in a few."

I barely managed to turn my back before the tears started rolling down my face. Big, fat tears that echoed the size of my heartbreak. And my humiliation. I could hear soft splats as each weighty drop hit the sand. My only consolation was that, as I trudged desolately across the beach, my bathing suit bottoms remained securely in place.

At least the resin stuck by me.

I unrolled the watertight seal of my dry bag and pulled out my sunscreen, journal, and beach towel. I spread the towel across a random patch of sand and dropped down on top of it. Something sharp bit into my thigh through the towel, but I didn't care.

The man I loved was hooking up with another girl last night?! But his Ikea eyes had lovingly caressed *my* face. It was *my* hand he held, *my* lips he kissed, and *my* aid he rushed to in a time of crisis.

Me he promised to call. AND DIDN'T. Because he was busy hooking up with some person named Angelika?! No. NO. It defied belief.

Tess appeared at the edge of my towel. "Hey, how's your day been? What are you writing—what's wrong?"

I buried my face in my hands and asked, "Was Tristan having sex with some girl named Angelika last night under a pool table?"

Tess sighed and dropped down in the sand beside me. She draped a sweaty arm around my shoulders. "They told you that?" she asked, nodding toward the Chatty Cathies at the other end of the beach.

"Uh-huh," I sniffled. "Is it true?"

"Probably."

I looked up at her in amazement.

"What? You want me to lie?" She shrugged. "Tristan's . . . Tristan. He'll nail anything that moves. And he's pretty enough that anything that moves mostly lets him."

Welcome to Find Out Island, population: me. My eyes were open so wide I'm surprised the upper lids didn't flip inside out. If only they'd been that way last week.

"Why didn't you tell me?" I demanded.

"I didn't think I'd need to after he ditched you drunk on the beach."

I shook my head. "That was my fault. I didn't know about coconut rum. And he was so nice about the whole thing!"

She looked skeptical. "*And* after he ignored your calls and texts for days."

"I just, I don't know. I've never seen him holding a phone. I thought maybe he liked to be present in his life . . ." I trailed off, realizing how dumb that sounded.

Tess looked distressed. "Look, Caitlin, if I'd realized—"

"No," I interrupted, "it's okay. It's nothing." My anguish was nothing. Well, nothing that wouldn't wait for later, anyway. "Right now," I took a deep breath, "right now I need to find Tristan."

"Oh, sweetie." Her arm tightened around my shoulders. "That's not a good idea. If you're looking for closure or something, you won't get it. He just—"

"No, I *need* to find Tristan," I repeated. "Not for closure. Okay, not *just* for closure," I amended. "I have to find out what happened to that bale."

Tess looked pained. "Yeah, I guess you do," she agreed. She studied me for a long moment, then sighed. "I think he's on one of those catamarans. I'll text him."

As Tess tapped at her screen, I began repacking my things in my dry bag. When I came to my bottle of sunscreen, I let out a tiny sob and spiked it into the sand.

SPF 70 does nothing to protect against heartache.

Aboard *Xanadu*
Roaming charges be damned
7:41 p.m., August 25

First, I called Shelby. In times of crisis, a girl needs her best friend.

"Oh my god, finally!" she shrieked. "I only sent you three hundred texts!"

"I KNOW," I said. "I mean, wait. What?"

"I cannot believe she did this," she ranted. "I know she thinks sugar is poison, but Lord's sake, that woman has *lost* the plot."

"Uhhhh"—my brain scrambled for a frame of reference—"what?"

"This weekend?" she said, in a tone that strongly implied I should know what she was talking about.

"Uh . . ."

"The Oxford Regatta?" she prompted again. Her voice had gone dangerously quiet.

"Oh," I said heavily, suddenly remembering. Shelby had aged out of Optis in May. This was her first regatta skippering a 420. She'd been practicing with her new crew all summer. "Right. How is that going?"

"HOW DO YOU THINK?" Her voice was not quiet now.

"Um. Not . . . great?" I guessed hesitantly.

There came a long pause, then, "Did you *read* my *texts*?"

"Well . . ."

"No, Caitlin," she ground out, "it is *not* going great because my mom caught me making microwave cake-in-a-mug and LOST HER MIND and now I'm GROUNDED."

Oh, holy shrimp.

"She won't drive me to Oxford and my dad is out of town, so there's nothing he can do about it until he gets back. And now she knows we have sugar in the house, and she found it and threw it away. *But*," she continued, "I appreciate you *finally* responding to my texts."

"I . . . I—"

Shelby gasped. "*Wait.* Wait one genuflecting minute. Is that even why you're calling? I thought you said you couldn't call."

"Ummmm . . ."

"UNBELIEVABLE." I was suddenly very glad for the 1,500 miles between us. "Did you even call to check on me? Is this *all about you*? AGAIN?!"

"No!" I cried. I mean, maybe, yes? I guess? Oof. Okay. My bad. "Shelby?"

But the line was dead.

Yikes. That development wasn't just bad, it was superbad. But that was a problem for Tomorrow Caitlin. Or maybe even Next Week Caitlin. And I needed guidance now.

I suppose it's a blessing that I have such a keen memory for numbers. I picked up my phone once more and dialed the number that Mrs. Brandon, my eighth and tenth grade religion teacher, had instructed us to call if we were ever in trouble. I never really liked Mrs. Brandon. She made all the girls in my class take Mary as their confirmation names because she thought we were all picking cool names, like Blaise and Aquilina, for the "wrong reasons." Also, whenever a topic even tangentially related to family life came up, she would fix the class with her grim stare and pronounce, "You know, not everyone gets *the Gerber baby*."

Oh, and she said birth control pills would kill us.

But she made us all memorize this number, just in case, so maybe she wasn't all bad.

"Hello," a youthful female voice answered promptly. "Thank you for calling The Heart Line."

"Hi," I said despondently.

"I'm so glad you called. How are you feeling tonight?"

"Like I'm on fire," I moaned.

"Do you need medical assistance?" she asked.

"No, it's fine," I sighed. All the medical technology in the world won't cure sunburn. I can feel the melanomas forming on my shoulders even as I write.

Oh, wait. Those are blisters. *Gross.*

"Okay, let's talk about why you called. You're in trouble?" the voice prompted.

Omg, if only she knew. "*So* much trouble." I poked at one of the bigger blisters.

"Have you decided what you're going to do?"

"Umm." You know, I had no idea blisters could be so clear. This one looked just like a little moonstone—firm, and smooth, and kind of pearly.

"So you're undecided. Good. Do you know about your options?"

"Huh?" The more I rubbed the blister, the looser the skin got. I decided to leave it alone before I accidentally popped it. "Honestly, I'm all out of options."

"No, no!" her voice burst through the connection, trembling with earnestness. "You always have options. I'm here to help."

Great, but how, exactly, was she going to do that? "Look, can we just get to the part where you make me feel better?"

"Yes, of course. Tell me how you're feeling."

"Humiliated," I said. "Angry. Heartbroken. Assaulted. Burned. Duped."

"Were you hurt by someone?"

"Yes!"

"How did it happen?"

"I was just trying to find out what he'd done with the pot, and he totally perved on me."

"I'm sorry?"

"Oh, forget it," I said. How could Hotline Girl possibly understand? All she could do was parrot lines off her stupid script. Besides, I was starting to feel guilty about the roaming charges. My bougie new allowance wouldn't stretch forever. "I'm gonna have to let you go now."

"No, listen." The lady sounded urgent. "God has a plan for you."

This was such a weird conversation. "Really?" I said skeptically. "He seems like more of a pantser."

"Did you know babies have a heartbeat at just six weeks of gestation?"

I froze in horror as it all clicked into place. No. She *didn't*. I mean, for crying out loud! I jerked the phone away from my face and gave it a fierce glare. I hoped Mrs. Brandon's hair caught fire and all her grandchildren married Unitarians. "That's not even true!" I yelled into the phone. "Stop lying to vulnerable people and get a real job!"

I ended the call on her gasp and flopped back on the bunk.

I am fully aware this is all my own stupid fault. I mean, I should have known that any guy who would abandon his date on a beach, any guy who would fool around with random girls beneath other people's pool tables—well, any guy like that would also have an ulterior motive for helping me out in a time of crisis.

"Hi, gorgeous," he greeted when he at last strolled up, munching on a bag of chips. "How are you?"

Tess gave him a disgusted look. Having done her part by texting him, she tucked her phone back in her pocket, gave my shoulder a pat, and strode off across the beach.

"Can we talk?" I forced myself to meet his eyes. It wasn't so bad. It was like I had immunity now to his evil vampire charms. "In private?"

His face stretched in a slow grin. "Absolutely."

There were no private spots available on the beach, so Tristan borrowed a dinghy from that Cameron guy and we motored across the sound to The Bitter End.

The Bitter End was closed, of course, locked down and buttoned up for the season, so instead of going all the way in to their dinghy dock, Tristan tied up to a wide, wooden swim platform that was anchored in the middle of their mooring field. As I stepped up onto the platform, it shifted slightly under my weight, then lurched more sharply as Tristan stepped on.

He caught me as I stumbled and didn't let go.

"I've missed you," he murmured, moving in for a kiss.

I squirmed and pushed at the same time. "Tristan, wait."

His arms tightened and he pulled me closer against his body, and I felt something. Was that a vape pen or—oh my god! Was that his . . . *pulsing manhood*?! GROSS.

"I've been thinking about you all week," he said.

I squirmed harder. "Even when you were under that pool table with Angelika?"

"Don't be like that," he breathed damply into my ear. Was this supposed to be sexy? Because I am all out of appreciation for hot, humid air, particularly when it smells like Spicy Doritos.

"You shouldn't believe everything you hear," he went on.

"Yeah," I shoved harder, "like anything that comes out of *your* mouth. Let me go!"

Holding the back of my head with one hand, he held me still while he ground his mouth over mine. Then, with his free hand, he reached between us and honked my boob. *Honked.* Like a horn on a beach cruiser!

Believe it or not, it was the boob-honking that saved me. And the yellow bikini. Because, as much respect as I have for the aesthetic benefits of artful padding, it does *not* feel like a boob.

Tristan jerked his mouth away from mine and looked down in confusion. Which is when I brought my hands up and, just like they taught us in health class last year, slammed my cupped palms down over his ears.

"Fooey!" he yelled. (Yeah, not really. That's for Grandma again.) "You impertinent little hoyden!" (Still for Grandma.)

"You kiss every girl on the island with that mouth?" I asked, retreating to the far side of the swim platform.

"This is why I flipping (Grandma.) hate American girls!" he snapped. "Don't even pretend you don't want it. You're *desperate* for it. You've been calling my house for days. You asked me to bring you someplace private."

"Yeah, to *talk*!" I yelled, waving my arms. "You're *disgusting*. I just want to know about the bale!"

"What *about* the bale?" he huffed.

"I need you to tell me exactly where you left it. It wasn't behind the chicken shed."

He laughed, and not very nicely either.

"Seriously, Tristan. The guys who left it on my boat, they want it back." I took a deep breath. "I appreciate that you took certain risks helping me out, but I really need to find that bale. These guys are serious and they have a flare gun, and if they survived the lemur attack, they're going to come looking for their stuff again. I have to get it back to them ASAP."

"Ah ha-ha-ha." He actually pointed at me while he laughed. Very mature.

"Tristan." I crossed my arms over my chest. "What did you do with it?"

"Oh," he said, pretending to wipe tears of laughter from his eyes, "this is too good."

It was then I realized that it is possible for even someone as beautiful as Tristan to look . . . ugly. I also noticed that, at some point, his Prince Harry accent had vanished and now he sounded just like everyone else around here. Was *anything* about this guy for real?

"What happened to it?" I demanded frantically. "Did you *smoke it* or something?"

He chuckled. "Even I can't smoke that much weed. I shared it with a few friends."

For the second time that day, my heart stopped.

My throat ached with the need to shout, but all I could get out was a hoarse whisper. "You what?" I cleared my throat and tried again. "YOU DID *WHAT*?"

"Hey," he glared, "I did you a favor. I told everyone who I got it from. They're all very grateful. Now you have friends."

So that's why everyone on the beach was so happy to see me? They all thought I was some kind of drug fairy?

"You equine behind," I said. (Grandma.) "You parent-honoring sibling in Christ." (Or something like that.)

"You know what," he fumed, "I don't have to listen this."

And here's where I made my mistake. You see, he was standing right by the dinghy—and I wasn't. He didn't waste time starting the engine, just hopped in and shoved off from the swim platform with a massive push. Within seconds he'd drifted farther than I could jump. I tried anyway and, falling short, plunged deep into the cool, blue water. I surfaced and swam after him as fast as I could, but he gave the pull start a furious yank and, an instant later, was sputtering off toward the far side of the sound.

I supposed I should be thankful he didn't run me over on his way back to the party. A propeller can do catastrophic things to the human body.

As I hauled myself, dripping, back onto the platform, I screamed after him, "You two-timing, puss-sucking, cheese-breathed, pencil-dicked *asshole*!"

Sorry, Grandma. He deserved it.

~~~~~~~~~~~~~~

It was several hours before Tess realized I hadn't returned to the beach with Tristan. I spent the whole time sitting on that stupid swim platform, broiling away in the afternoon sun.

I guess I could have swum over to the beach at the Bitter End and found some shade, but sometimes things across the water look closer than they really are. The beach wasn't near enough for me to feel perfectly comfortable with the distance, and I also worried that no one would think to look for me at a deserted resort. At least I had high visibility going for me, stranded as I was on a floating dock in the middle of an empty mooring field.

It was probably the right decision. Tess and Jonas found me right away, once they noticed I was missing. Of course, by the time they borrowed Cameron's dinghy (that kid lends his dinghy out like a Netflix password) and rode to the rescue, I was completely fried. I protected my face by lying on my stomach, taking most of the damage on my dorsal side. And, by four o'clock, the sun had dipped low enough that I could sit and stand upright, with my back to the sun, and keep the front of my body shaded.

I know I should be grateful for small gifts, and I am happy my face isn't a blistery mess. But, as I've never been a stomach sleeper, this is going to make for a very uncomfortable night.

But even after all that had transpired, the Day of Disasters was not over.

When we got back to *Xanadu*, Jonas carefully helped me out of the dinghy and onto the boat. Even moving very slowly, it stung a lot. He offered to lift me out, which would have spared me having to bend my legs, but with approximately fifty percent of my skin crisping up like a pork rind, there was really no good place from which to lift.

"Let's get you out of that bikini and into a T-shirt or something," Tess offered, leading me into the cabin. "I brought a really soft sundress you can borrow."

"That'd be awesome," I said gratefully.

She handed me the dress, and I stepped into the head to change.

"Tess?" I called a minute or so later. "Um. I have a little problem."

I unlocked the door. Tess squeezed inside, and I showed her.

"What *happened*?" she gasped.

"The suit tends to ride up," I explained. "I dripped a little resin on it so it would stay put."

Her jaw gaped, and we stared at each other for a long moment.

"You cemented your bathing suit to your butt," she said wonderingly.

"It's two-part resin. I didn't add any catalyst. I don't know why it's like this!"

She just stood there gawking at me, her face aghast.

"I thought it would stay gluey," I moaned.

I could see it in her eyes, that exact moment it clicked for her that this wasn't a joke; that this was a thing I, a real person who is not even new to this planet, had actually done to myself. She *exploded* laughing. "You cemented you bathing suit to your butt!" she hooted.

"She *what*?" came a voice from the other side of the door.

"Tess! *Shhhh!*" I urged miserably. My entire body tingled with mortification. Or maybe that was the sunburn. Who could tell?

"I'm sorry, I'm sorry." Still giggling, she held up a placating hand. "Okay, so . . . I guess we'll have to cut it off."

I whimpered mournfully.

"It's a cute bathing suit and all, but we can find you another," she consoled.

I was thinking more about how it was going to feel cutting bikini bottoms off my deep-fried backside.

"Don't panic," she instructed. "I'll go get us some scissors."

This statement was misleading. She didn't *go* anywhere. What she actually did was crack the door open, pop her head through the gap, and shout, "Someone find me some scissors," at the three guys milling curiously around the cabin. Then she pulled her head back inside and closed the door.

"Hey." There came a thumping at the door. "What are you two doing in there? Anything we'd want to know about?"

"Scissors, Lucas," she called in a sing-song voice. "Knock when you got 'em."

Eventually, the guys did come through with a pair of scissors. Tess gave them a quick wash, as they smelled like they might have come from a tackle box, and started snipping. While she worked, I concentrated on not thinking about all the fishy bacteria that could be migrating to my bloodstream through my raw epidermis.

"Okay," she announced finally. "I've cut as much fabric as I can, but the rest is . . . well, it's glued to your butt. Do you want me to just leave it?"

"No," I started to shake my head, but froze when the tight, crispy skin on the back of my neck screamed at the movement. "It's not like I'll be lying around on my back anyway. Just pull it off."

She did just as I asked. It wasn't as bad as I thought it'd be—or as successful. Under tension, the scraps of bathing suit pulled free while the resin stuck fast to the skin.

"I'm sure it'll wear off," Tess said. "I mean, sooner or later it'd have to, right?"

"God," I said.

She helped me into her sundress, which was several sizes too big for me but soft as promised, then gathered all the bikini scraps she could find and stuffed them in my backpack.

"Tess?"

"Yeah?"

"Do we have to tell anyone about this?"

"Well, I won't breathe a word," she informed me, "but . . ." She opened the door to reveal Enzo and Lucas, doubled over in silent laughter. Jonas, standing in the galley, had his head shoved down into the dry storage compartment, but his shoulders were shaking suspiciously.

"I don't think I'll have to," she finished.

~~~~~~~~~~

After twenty minutes or so, everyone quit laughing at me and expressed some concern for my condition. Enzo dug through the contents of the glass-fronted refrigerator and came up with some aloe vera gel (the good kind, that's laced with lidocaine.) I stretched out on one of the bench seats in the cockpit and let Tess cover me in green gel.

I've never been more miserable in my whole fifteen—I mean sixteen—years of life. My back is fried, and my butt is covered with flakes of resin. The guy I thought liked me doesn't—and he's a sleazy sack of lemur poo. Every kid on the island thinks I'm their "connection," except for these four who, after today, probably won't want anything to do with me. They've had a pretty choice view of the old Caitlin for most of the afternoon. I don't even know where New Caitlin is. I think I might have left her on that swim platform. Oh, and somewhere out there are two lemur-bitten drug smugglers who are never getting their bale back.

I've got problems.

Enzo walked out of the cabin and said, "There's a big cookout on the beach. If you don't feel like coming, we can bring you back some food."

I cast my eyes up at the evening sky. The moon on the rise was half-empty. "Just leave me here," I moaned into the seat cushion.

And they did.

CHAPTER 15

Aboard *Xanadu*
Prop walk of shame
10:47 a.m., August 26

This morning, I am no closer to recovering New Caitlin than I was last night.

I awoke to the sound of Tess snoring lightly on the opposite settee. Morning light filtered through the ports and nothing loud was happening, so I surmised the twins were also asleep. No surprise there. Everyone who *wasn't* too sunburned to move had spent the night partying on the beach, swimming beneath the summer moon, and enjoying their last chance to cut loose before school starts. I rolled painfully off the settee where I'd slept and staggered out of the cabin.

Jonas sat alone in the cockpit, reading a paperback.

"Good morning," he said, glancing up.

"Hi," I returned. I kept my gaze firmly fixed on the cover of his book, avoiding eye contact. The shame of yesterday will never leave me.

"You want some breakfast?" he asked. "You missed dinner last night."

"Sure," I said dully, not really caring. Why eat when my life is ruined?

I followed him back into the cabin and watched as he pulled boxes of pastries and cereal out of the dry locker. I pointed to a box at random and, because I was pretty sure I couldn't move without my skin splitting asunder and my entrails spilling out, he poured Lucky Charms into a bowl for me, added milk, and handed me a spoon.

We went back out on deck, and I gingerly perched on the edge of the padded bench seat.

"About your turtle box—" I began.

He waved his hand at me dismissively. "Nah. I'll make another one."

I thought about that for a moment. If he was starting over, I might have a few ideas about the design of the casing. And the controls. "Can I help?"

He grinned and shook his head at me but didn't answer.

A quiet settled over us as the boat swung gently on its mooring. Jonas gazed out over the sound, and I munched on red hearts, green clovers, and blue moons. A puff of breeze funneled through the hatch in the windscreen and lashed my hair against the sensitive skin of my back. I winced and continued chewing.

"It'll get better," he said softly. I don't think he was talking about my sunburn.

A passing seagull, spying my cereal, veered close and gave a sharp cry. I jerked in surprise and came in full contact with the back of the bench seat. My eyes watered and I hissed in pain.

"I doubt it," I said tightly.

Around 10:45, Tess and the twins rolled out of the cabin.

"Jonas, will you make us breakfast?" Enzo implored.

Jonas rolled his eyes. "It's almost lunchtime. Have some cereal."

Enzo recoiled. "*Cereal?* I only just went to bed and this one"—he pointed at Tess—"has cruelly interrupted my sleep cycle. I need a proper breakfast. I need eggs. I need sausage!"

"And dumb bread," Lucas added, yawning hugely. "Did you bring dumb bread?"

"Maybe you two should go to sleep earlier," Tess told them.

Enzo looked affronted. "We're half Brazilian! They'd revoke our citizenship if we went to bed before dawn."

Jonas said something about dumb bread and Tupperware, and Enzo disappeared back into the cabin.

"Bring me one!" Lucas called after him, then turned to me. "And how's our crispy critter this morning?"

I bared my teeth.

Tess clapped her hands. "Okay, so, what's everyone want to do today?" she asked. She seemed to be avoiding my eyes.

Lucas yawned. "Take a nap." His voice sounded lower than usual and rather scratchy.

"You just woke up."

He shrugged and plopped down beside me on the bench seat. "What time does the market open? Do you think they sell aspirin?"

Tess pursed her lips. "What about you, Jonas?"

Enzo reappeared, munching on something that looked like a large, square scone. He threw a matching pastry at his brother, who groaned and caught it. "Ooo, gooh," he said, spraying crumbs across the cockpit. He swallowed with an audible gulp. "Are we making plans?"

Jonas held up his book. "I'm going to read a bit."

"Ugh," Enzo grunted. "Fine. Tess?"

"Maybe a hike?" she asked.

I experienced a brief but terrifying goat flashback.

Enzo shot her a scornful look. "I don't hike."

"Okay, well, how about we go see the lemurs?" she proposed.

"NO!" Jonas and I both shouted.

"Hmph," she said, sounding miffed. "In that case, I think I'll lie in the sun and rest my eyes for a bit."

"How is that different from napping?" Lucas demanded.

Enzo dismissed them and zeroed in on me. "What about you, then? What do *you* want to do? We have an eFoil. Have you ever eFoiled? I could teach you." He practically vibrated with enthusiasm.

I stared at him incredulously.

"Enzo," Jonas said patiently, "she can barely move. Calm down and chew your food."

"Well, if you're all going to be like that," Enzo pouted, "then we might as well head home."

Tess shrugged. "Okay."

"Fine," I said, relieved.

"Do I have to be awake for that?" asked Lucas.

Jonas got up and started the engines. "No, you do not."

The Pickled Pirate
Circling the bowl
4:50 p.m., August 26

One night last fall, Shelby and I watched a movie called *Heathers*—not the series remake, but the original. It's a high school movie from the 1980s, so frizzy hair and shoulder pads feature heavily, and it stars a bunch of people I'd mostly never heard of before. Some seriously wild stuff happens in that movie but at one point, the heroine, Veronica, turns to her friend and says, "If you were happy every day of your life, you wouldn't be a human being. You'd be a game show host."

Well, I have now proven beyond a shadow of a doubt that I, Caitlin Davies, am not a game show host. Because I AM NOT HAPPY.

Of course, that's glass-half-empty thinking there, isn't it? That's the kind of thinking my mom would describe as "self-defeating." So let's not dwell on all that I am not; let's focus instead on what I *am*.

I *am* fifteen years old. This is good because, if statistics hold true, I will live two years longer than Tristan. This means that when he dies, I can go to his funeral and drive a stake through his wicked heart so that he may never rise again. Yay.

I *am* Catholic, so according to Mrs. Brandon, when I myself die (two years after Tristan), I will go straight to heaven, where I will binge-watch the catalogues of all the premium streaming services with the angels and saints, my dad, and possibly my brother (though it's not looking good for him); I will visit my mom and all her Druid buddies in purgatory; and I will send Christmas cards to Tristan as he rots in hell.

I *am* an object of ridicule. See yesterday's journal entries.

I *am* sunburned. And starting to peel.

And finally . . .

I *am* homeless. Yes, you read that right. Homeless. I know. It was a surprise to me, too. Because, honestly, as the *Xanadu* sped back toward Soper's Hole, it never occurred to me that anything else could possibly go wrong. I was bruised, burned, demoralized, and movement-impaired. The blister on my shoulder (the one that looked like a moonstone) popped when we hit a big wave and my chin slammed down on it. And as my tender back forced me to lie stomach-down on the bench seat while the boat was underway, I was stuck listening to the twins bicker the whole way home.

"What's this rash on my foot, do you think? It's just gone a bit oozy."

"Looks like gangrene to me."

"I know you think you're being funny, but I don't even know what that *is*."

This, on top of everything else, was a lot to take. They argued about Lucas's athlete's foot for *half an hour*. In self-defense, I concentrated hard on ignoring them. I had to protect what little sanity

I had left. By the time we rounded the corner into Soper's Hole, my mental bulkheads were all but sealed to external stimuli. So it didn't immediately register when Lucas said, "Hey, look at all that smoke."

Or when Enzo said, "Did the ferry catch fire again?"

But when Jonas came sprinting back from the bow, shouting, "Caitlin, your boat is burning!" Well, that I noticed.

"Oh, my god. Where's your family?" Tess asked in alarm.

"They're staying at The Pickled Pirate," I recalled with relief. Good thing we'd discovered the through-hull issue before the wiring problems reared their incendiary heads.

Now that I think about it, it's pretty remarkable that Jonas could tell it was *Island Time* on fire, because all I could make out was billowing smoke, greedy flames, and great jets of water being pumped into the whole mess from the nearby fire boat. I couldn't see anything that identified it as *my* boat.

And then it sank.

And now it just looks like the tippy-top of a mast, sticking out of the water at a drunken angle. The wind-indicator is still attached to the top. Whenever a puff of wind rolls through, the little arrow spins around to point in the appropriate direction.

It reminds me of those sundials you sometimes see on gravestones.

The harbor master says we have a week to get the *Island Time* out of the way, because it poses a hazard to navigation. When the salvage guys come to raise it, I wonder if it will matter that the hull is barnacle free. I wonder if it will matter that the toe-rail is sanded smooth, and the bilge is daisy fresh, and the cushions on the settees are brand new. I wonder if it will matter that my books are still aboard, and Finn's Power Rangers, and my mom's witchy whisk broom. I wonder if *any* of this will matter.

I'm betting it won't.

The Pickled Pirate
Eating breakfast at the bar
8:06 a.m., August 27

I 'm back to eating breakfast with Finn at The Pickled Pirate. Need
I say more?

Although, due to our recent tragedy, the kitchen ladies have also
made a Mickey waffle for me this morning. As if a rodent-shaped
waffle could really distract me from the fact that I am now a friend-
less, homeless waif, adrift in a fickle, popularity-obsessed world.

Which reminds me: now I will never know if Persephone was
able to convince Blade the Buccaneer to embrace forgiveness and
start a new life with her in the Colonies. Poor, burned-up, sunken
Rebellious Passion. If only I had left you to molder in the book swap,
you'd still be with us today.

Mmmm. Wow. Who'd have thought? The ears really *do* taste
better.

The Pickled Pirate
Still at the bar
8:50 a.m., August 27

W hen the phone behind the bar rang, Bertrand answered like
usual, listened for a minute, then held the receiver out for me
to take.

"Hello?" I said, surprised but hopeful. I hadn't heard anything from Tess—she'd completely avoided me on the boat ride
home yesterday by pretending to nap. Only when I peeked inside
the cabin, she wasn't napping at all; she was reading Enzo's *Hello!*
magazine. And since we got back, she hadn't answered any of my
texts. I couldn't blame her for not wanting to speak to me—a case

of freakishness this severe might very well be contagious—but that didn't mean I wasn't bummed about it. I guess that's the downside of making friends under false pretenses. When New Caitlin backslides into the old Caitlin, the jig is up.

It wasn't Tess, though.

"This Caitlin?" a man's voice asked gruffly.

I glanced over at Bertrand, who watched me surreptitiously while sanitizing the TV remote.

"Yes," I said hesitantly.

"Heyyyy," the voice drawled, "we just wanted to say we're really sorry about your boat."

"Who is this?" I asked.

"We're your . . . friends. You know, the ones from Lemur Land."

My mouth opened in a silent scream. The smugglers! I'd forgotten all about them. Great, now I could be homeless *and* hunted by murderous criminals.

"Listen," I said, "I couldn't get your stuff back. I tried. I really did. But it's been . . . redistributed. And partially consumed, I think? It's unrecoverable. But," I continued earnestly, "I'd be happy to give you the name of the guy who lost it all."

"Hey, don't worry about it," said the voice.

"His name is Tristan Yancy, that's Y-A-N-C—what?"

"Don't worry about it," he repeated. "We appreciate you trying to get it back and all, and in light of your good faith efforts, we've decided to put this all behind us."

"Really?" I couldn't believe my luck. "Why?"

"Why what?"

"Why are we putting this all behind us?" I know, I should have quit while I was ahead, but this was not the way drug dealers usually operate (not in movies, anyway). I just wanted to make sure they didn't think I was in their debt or anything. I don't want to owe these kinds of people any favors. They'd probably make me be a drug mule, and I can't even swallow an aspirin, much less a balloon filled with cocaine.

There was a brief silence. "We just figured, after what happened yesterday, we're square now."

"Oh," I said. Then, "Wait, what happened yesterday?"

"Your boat burned up," he said impatiently.

"Yeeahhhhh . . . okayyyy . . ." A thought occurred to me. "So why would that make us square?"

This time the silence lasted almost ten seconds. "Like I said, we're really sorry about your boat."

"I got that part. *Why* are you sorry about my boat?" I demanded.

I heard muffled voices, and there was some crackling in the receiver, then a different voice came through the line.

"Okay, here's what happened," said the new voice, and I'm pretty sure it was Bald Guy. "When we came back to collect our missing *stuff*, we saw there was nobody on the boat, so we thought we'd go aboard and have another look around. You know, just in case you hadn't been straight with us. And while we were searching, we found something *else* we'd left, because we'd hidden it really good, inside the casing for the autopilot."

So I guess I should be glad we never had occasion to need the autopilot.

He continued, "We're talking a *full* box of Cohibas here, 400 bucks a pop and impossible to get outside Cuba or Spain. So we sat down on the settee to have a smoke, and, you know, those new cushions you guys sprang for are a lot nicer than the old ones. And then maybe we dozed off."

I gasped. Bertrand gave me a wild-eyed look.

"And Nathaniel dropped his cigar on the settee."

In the background, Nathaniel protested, "Nuh uh, man, that was *your* cigar! I put mine out in that little red robot helmet, remember?"

"And boy, lemme tell you, those new synthetic materials go up like lightning. Nathaniel and I barely made it out alive."

"Tell her about your shirt," I heard Nathaniel urge.

"Oh, yeah. It burned a hole in my favorite shirt."

"The one with mermaids?" I asked faintly.

"Yeah. I've had that shirt since college. Such a drag. Anyway, just wanted to let you know we're square now. 'Kay? Good talk. Bye now."

"No!" I yelled before he could hang up.

"No?" Bald Guy sounded startled.

"No." I said firmly. "You burned up my boat. You owe me."

We negotiated for several minutes until a settlement was reached, then bid each other polite farewells. I handed the bar phone back to Bertrand and sat for a while, staring at my hands and processing.

The *Island Time* did not randomly catch fire due to faulty wiring, or act of god, or any of the other causes we'd considered; nooooo, it was *negligently set aflame* by VIOLENT POT FIENDS.

And it's all my fault.

If I'd handled this differently, if I hadn't trusted Tristan to hide the pot (or at all), if I'd personally carried it to the chicken shed to ensure safe delivery . . . Or maybe, I don't know, if I hadn't tried to handle it myself, maybe if I'd just told my dad what was going on.

If I'd told my dad what was going on, we might still have a place to live.

CHAPTER 16

The Pickled Pirate
It's good for the soul
11:38 a.m., August 27

I didn't have to look far for my dad. He'd long since commandeered one of the corner dining tables as his own. There was a smattering of paperwork in front of him—police reports and faxes from our yacht broker—and he was discussing an appraisal with someone on his cell. His cheeks were stubbled and his eyes were tired.

I took an empty chair (carefully, because my back is still tender) and waited for him to finish his call.

"What's up?" he sighed, setting his phone on the table. "You need some money? Your mother says she's going shopping in St. Thomas tomorrow to get us all a few more pairs of underwear, that kind of thing. You can go with her if you want."

"It's my fault the boat burned up," I blurted out.

"What?"

Enunciating each word with excruciating care, I repeated my sordid confession.

"How could it be your fault?" my dad scoffed. "Finn—now, *Finn* I'd like for it, if I didn't know he and your mother were off hugging trees when it all went down. But you? Come on, Caitie, you're the fire safety poster child. And you weren't even here when it happened."

"No," I said miserably, "but my drug connections were."

He blinked. "Say that again?"

So I told him the whole story: about bilge cleaning, and Nathaniel and Bald Guy, and the *stuff*, and Tristan, and the flaming settee cushions. I left Jonas, Tess, and the twins out of it. They hadn't done anything, so there was no need to implicate them in my nightmare, but everything else? I laid it all out.

"And now," I concluded, "our boat's burned up with all our stuff on it, and sunk, and I'm *really* sorry."

My dad stared at me in shock.

I added desolately, "It's all my fault."

"Well," he said, looking pale, "yeah, it kind of is."

I started to cry.

"Why didn't you *tell* me?" he asked, scrubbing his hands over his face.

"I thought you'd get in *trouble!*" I wailed. "I thought you'd go to the police, and they'd be suspicious of you because we're live-aboards, and you'd end up deported, or in jail, or worse!"

"What's worse than jail?" he asked, looking shocky. He gave his head a brisk shake. "Forget it. Caitlin, you're *fifteen* years old. I know we let you take on a lot of responsibility for someone your age—mostly because you seem to like it—but there are some things that you are not prepared to handle. You should *not* be associating with smugglers and drug dealers. You should *not* be making decisions about what is best for this family. You are *not* the parent here. *I* am," he said sternly. Then, almost as an afterthought, he added, "And so is your mother."

"I *know*," I sobbed.

"No," he said, "I don't think you do. But maybe you're starting to get the idea."

"I'm sorry," I moaned.

He sighed. "Look, you should have come to me about all this, but it's not *really* your fault the boat is gone. You don't control the world. You aren't accountable for the actions of criminals. You aren't accountable for the actions of anybody but yourself, okay?"

"Like it matters," I sniffed. "We're still homeless."

"No, we're not." He waved his hand at the bar. "We have The Pickled Pirate. And in a week or two, we'll have a very nice check from West Indies Insurers."

My jaw dropped. "What?!"

"Yeah, we're insured based on the survey the seller originally provided to our yacht broker. The one *you* demanded they supply. So we'll get another boat. A better boat." He gave me a wry smile. "Maybe even a boat with a third cabin."

It took me a moment to process that.

A better boat.

My own cabin.

If I'd known about this, I might have burned the thing up myself. Except . . .

"But what about all our stuff?" I asked. "All Finn's toys, and our clothes, and Erica's New Age Druid crap?" (My grandma will have thrown this book in the trash by now.)

He shrugged. "It's just stuff. We'll get more." He reached over and squeezed my shoulder. Ouch. "It's not the stuff that matters anyway. We're all safe. We have each other. And you have all those new friends you've been making."

I shook my head. "I don't think so."

"Why not?"

So then I had to tell him about New Caitlin—or the demise of New Caitlin, I should say. I gave him the whole pathetic, mortifying tale.

"Jeez, you just never can tell what's going on in there," he marveled, giving my head a pat. "Maybe that's a good thing. Caitlin, you are ridiculous. And so is your friend Shelby. Why would you even try to change yourself? There's nothing wrong with you."

"Yeah, right!" This from the man who'd just agreed that, at the very least, my actions *contributed* to the epic destruction of the family home. Talk about inconsistent. No wonder I'm so screwed up. "They'll never speak to me again. I'm a pariah."

"Oh, yeah?" He nodded at something behind me. "Take a look at that."

I carefully pivoted in my chair.

"Hi, Caitlin," Tess said, tentatively.

My dad offered her a chair, then gathered up his papers and strolled over to the bar.

"Hi," I said.

"I was hoping to talk to you," she explained, "but if you don't really want to talk to me, I'll understand."

I gaped at her. "Why would *I* not want to talk to *you?*"

"Because everything that happened to you yesterday? It was *my* fault. If it weren't for me, Tristan would never have found out about the bale. I didn't tell him, I swear!" she said hurriedly, seeing my face, "But I told my older sister about it on FaceTime, and I didn't realize it then, but Tristan overheard."

"Ohhh," I said. Events in my head rearranged themselves based on this new information.

"I didn't find out until last night at the beach," she went on anxiously. "I went up to Tristan, to kick his ass for treating you like that, and for ditching you on that swim dock. He told me the rest of it.

He *bragged* about it." She looked down at her hands. "And I'd been laughing at you, about your bathing suit bottoms. I feel so bad." She cocked her head to the side. "I mean, that *was* funny."

I gave her a look.

"But really insensitive," she finished.

I sighed. "I was the one who trusted him when any idiot could see what he was really like. You don't have anything to be sorry about."

"Really?"

"Except for the laughing at me part," I added.

She gave a watery giggle. "Here, I brought you some clothes to wear until you have a chance to go shopping. You can keep them. I outgrew them a few years ago."

"Thanks," I said dryly, accepting the loaded shopping bag she handed me. I glanced at the stuff on top. It all seemed to be smaller versions of Tess's current surf-hippy apparel. There was even a woven poncho.

My mom will be so pleased.

"So," she said, bracingly, "you want to come to yoga with me?"

"No," I said. *You have to draw the line somewhere.* "But I will ride over with you. There's something I need to do."

"Great." She glanced down at her phone. "I have time to help you buy turkey if you want. You're probably just forgetting to say 'good morning' before you order."

I blinked. "What?"

Tess made for the door. "You can't just walk up and demand turkey, you know. Manners are important around here."

It took a mere five minutes on the marina Wi-Fi to accomplish what I needed to. There was nothing mere about the cost, though. Seventy-five dollars a week. I was effectively broke for the next month. Really good apologies don't come cheap.

I exited my browser and tapped Shelby's name. This next bit was going to require some Finn-sitting because I hadn't figured out where the island's plasma collection center was located yet.

Shelby answered on the first ring. "To what do I owe the honor?" she asked in a chilly voice.

I gave a deep sigh. "I'm sending you cakes."

Silence.

"Caroline's Cakes."

Shelby gave a soft gasp.

"One a week for the next month. They'll be delivered to your dad's office. He's going to sneak them home and stash them in the minifridge in your garage apartment."

"Seven-layer caramel?"

"Two seven-layer caramels, two seven-layer chocolates," I confirmed.

"Oh my gahhhhhhhhd," Shelby breathed. "You're forgiven! You're my best friend again! How are you affording this? Did you start selling drugs or something?"

I groaned. "How about we talk about you? Are you un-grounded? What happened?"

"Yeah, Dad ungrounded me as soon as he got home. And when I told him about Mom throwing the sugar away, he was like, 'Ugh. I'll get more sugar. I'll put it in an oatmeal container or something so she won't find it.' So now we'll at least be able to make decent coffee again. But I missed all three days of the regatta."

"Was it any good?" I asked. "The mug cake?"

"I mean, it was kind of rubbery but, you know . . . cake."

I think there was probably a lesson somewhere in that statement, but I have no clue what it was.

The Pickled Pirate
The sun'll come out *mañana*
8:17 p.m., August 27

Tonight, I sat on the dinghy dock and watched the sun set, and you know what? It was beautiful. I never noticed before how quickly the sun sinks into the sea, how the islands become purple-gray shadows and the water turns to hammered copper. For the first time, I noticed the way the breeze gets just a little bit cooler at the end of the day.

Or maybe it *was* the first time the breeze got cooler at the end of the day. I still say August in the Caribbean sucks.

But anyway, as the sun dropped from sight and the sky glowed pink, I stared into the water, waiting for the fish to come out and start eating each other, and considered the lesson all of this has taught me.

Clearly, I was born under an uncool star. Despite a thoughtful and determined effort, New Caitlin ended up being just as much of a bust as the old one. Uncoolness dogs my every footstep. I don't know why I never it realized before: uncool is my copilot. Sorry, Jesus.

It's so obvious. I mean, duh, I'm a Leo, which I have it on good authority is the astrological sign commonly associated with perfectionism, bossiness, and naivete. Only the first applies to me, of course, but perfectionism is hardly the personality trait most likely to result in social success.

This could also explain why, when life finally tossed something cool my way, I didn't recognize him. I wasn't even particularly nice to cool. I ignored cool to chase after a perfidious pot-thief.

Lucky for me, cool is the patient sort.

"Hey, you good?" Jonas asked, dropping down gracefully to sit beside me on the dock. I'd texted him earlier and asked him to stop by.

"I've got something for you." I pointed to the maroon plaid carryall at my back.

His eyes lit. "Is that—"

"Yep," I confirmed.

He grabbed the bag by the handle and slid it closer. "How did you get it back?" he asked, unzipping the top and peering inside.

My final meeting with the Bald Guy and Gray Hair had been a brief one. They hadn't even gotten out of the car. In fact, they hadn't even come to a complete stop. "It wasn't a big deal," I said.

Jonas gave the carryall a quick hug and set it next to him. "Thank you. I'm very happy to have it back. I hope you didn't do anything foolish."

"No way. I had it all handled." Well, mostly handled. I hadn't expected them to toss the turtle box out the window like that. Fortunately, it was sturdily constructed.

"Well . . . that's good." His tone was a little dubious for my taste, but I let it go. He settled in and asked, "What are you reading?"

"Philosophy," I said.

He picked up my book and examined the cover. "This is a book on astrology."

"I know."

He shook his head and set the book down. Leaning back, he braced his arms behind him, and we watched the fish.

"How are you feeling?" he asked, turning his head and studying me with a gaze more perceptive than Blade the Buccaneer's on his best day.

"Not bad, considering."

"Considering your boat burned up?"

"And sank," I reminded him.

"And sank," he agreed.

"And considering I made an enormous, pathetic fool of myself," I elaborated.

"No, you didn't do that."

"Ha. Yes, I did. I can't believe you even want to talk to me anymore."

He eyed me curiously. "Why?"

"Because I'm a fake, an illusion—practically a grifter!"

"You seem real to me. And I don't know what a grifter is."

"It's like when Persephone was tricked into playing a rigged dice game with one of the deckhands and—you know what? It doesn't matter. Just trust me on this: I'm an enormous fake. The Caitlin you like does not exist."

He tipped his head to the side. "I still don't understand why you're a fake."

"Jonas," I said, waving my hands in frustration, "I'm not the cool, sophisticated girl you thought I was. That was an *act*. I'm not really like that at all. I'm really a cleaning-obsessed freak who hates parties and listens to the wrong kinds of music."

"Caitlin, I already know you like to clean. It's what you're doing *every time* I come see you. And I think you're very cool."

Well, that was nice of him to say. But, still.

"Nothing worked the way we thought it would," I shared.

"What didn't work? Who's *we*?" He sounded confused.

I guess it was confession time again. I told him all about my life back home (Leaving out the part about skipping third grade. A lady's age is private.) and Shelby's plan for me start over as a normal eleventh grader.

"How is resining a bathing suit to your butt *normal*?" he interrupted.

I couldn't believe he went there. I shot him a dark look and continued, "We thought, just for once, I should be the star of my own movie."

"That's not a very good plan," he commented mildly. "It's not even very original."

I wobbled my head in acknowledgement. "We watch a lot of TV."

He reached down, picked my hand up off the dock, and held it loosely in his own. He absently tapped our joined hands against his knee and seemed to consider the matter. "The kind of movies you and your friend watched," he said thoughtfully, "they usually show people getting popular because that's what most people want. But is that what *you* want?"

"Yeah." Duh.

"Really? Because if you were popular like in those movies, you'd have to go to parties all the time and hang out with people like Onessa and Viv."

"Well, if it's a choice between being a total freak all my life or going to a few parties and being normal, then I pick the parties."

He let out an exasperated breath. "Those aren't the only options, you know. Maybe we need a new metaphor." He scooted closer, until his left arm nudged my right shoulder, and the side of my leg was snugged up against his. "Look around," he instructed.

I did, then turned back to him expectantly.

"What do you see?"

"Boats. Jacks. The Pickled Pirate. Soper's Hole."

He nodded. "You know what this place was, a long time ago?"

"What?"

"A pirate hangout."

I gave a surprised laugh. "Really?"

"You see how the wind always comes from that direction?" he said, pointing at a dip in the mountain on the inner curve of the harbor.

"Yeah."

"Well, the pirates hung out here in Soper's Hole because, whenever they spotted the British Navy ships, they could hoist their sails and scream out of here on a downwind run, while the Navy was still tacking upwind toward the harbor."

"Awesome," I breathed, looking out over the harbor with new eyes. I could picture Blade the Buccaneer's ship perfectly, bobbing gently on its Boaty Ball, ready to haul the mail at the first sign of a Union Jack.

"And you know something about pirates?"

"Lots of things," I assured him.

He grinned. "One thing in particular, I mean."

"What?"

He gave me an intent look. "They weren't very popular. But they always got to be in charge."

I stared up at him.

"Maybe you don't need to be the star of your own movie. Maybe you need to be the captain of your own ship."

"What kind of ship?" I asked, curious where he was going with this.

He waved his hand. "It can be a pirate ship, or a navy ship, or a *cruise* ship. Or even a sunken ship." His gaze darted out to the tip of *Island Time*'s mast. "Look, it can be any kind of ship you want. You still get to be in charge."

"In charge," I said slowly, testing the sound of it. "I'm in charge."

He nodded. "As long as you're captain of a ship that suits you, you're in charge."

"Captain," I said. "I get to be captain."

He gave me a look of faint alarm. "I think I've created a monster."

"I think I've created a monster, *Captain*," I corrected.

"Mmm," he said noncommittally. "So does this mean you're over this New Caitlin stuff?"

"Yes," I answered, somewhat distracted. If I'm captain, I should get to wear a fancy hat.

"And, just out of curiosity, does Captain Caitlin need help figuring out the lyrics to 'Exodus'?"

"Oh," I winced. "You heard about that."

"I guess that was part of the whole New Caitlin thing?"

"Yeah. I do really like that song." I considered, "Although I'm thinking I misunderstood the lyrics."

"Guess so."

"But," I went on, "I like musicals, too. Particularly Muppet ones. I'm going to play a lot of those on my ship."

"Do I get a say in this?" he asked, leaning closer. His brown eyes sparkled in the light from the bar, and by our feet, water churned as a tarpon gobbled a fat minnow.

"Nope," I answered. "I'm in charge."

And then he didn't kiss me. But he will.

I have a plan.

ACKNOWLEDGMENTS

Caitlin's story would never have graced the printed page if not for the encouragement of Ryan Smernoff and Erica Downing; and that story would be very, very bad if not for the aid of my marvelous agent, Sarah Gerton; so cheers to you three! Thanks (and apologies) to the friends I ruthlessly drafted for their Caribbean expertise: Akeem Lennard, whose answers to all my BVI-specific questions frequently had me in stitches, and Erika Romer, who gave the manuscript a full read on a tight deadline, bless her. Thanks, also, to the wonderful friends who listened to me whine about this book: Kristen Blabey, Liz Young, Erica Downing (well, it's kind of your fault, isn't it?), Nikki Barthelmess, Heather Poet-Johnson (who read it *twice*—I don't deserve you, lady), Claudia Thorsen, Fabiana Acosta, D.J. Palladino, and especially Rae Castroll, who once met a girl rather like Caitlin and befriended her anyway.

Regan Edwards shared her tales from the charter industry trenches; Enzo and Lucas Acosta shared their names; Jason Worrell shared the best line in the book; Bruce McAlpin shared some great intel I unfortunately had to cut; and Jessica Ludy shared all her favorite jokes (now Tess's). I am extremely grateful to all of you!

And to Bryan Foscue-Boyd, who makes me happy every day of my life, makes the good times magical, the boring stuff fun, the awful stuff tolerable, and laughs with me about all of it: I love you.

ABOUT THE AUTHOR

ELIZABETH FOSCUE grew up in a house on a Florida bay and on a boat in the Caribbean Sea. A hurricane got the house, but the boat has fared better. She earned a BA in Linguistics from the University of Florida, then a JD and LLM from Georgetown University Law Center, and in the midst of all that got married in a church on a hill in the British Virgin Islands. A hurricane got the church, but the marriage has fared better. Elizabeth lives in Santa Barbara, California, with her husband and two awesome kiddos.